FINDING HER LOVE

Warren C. Holloway

GOOD 2 GO PUBLISHING

FINDING HER LOVE
Written by Warren C. Holloway
Cover Design: Davida Baldwin, Odd Ball Designs
Typesetter: Mychea
ISBN: 978-1-947340-66-4
Copyright © 2021 Good2Go Publishing
Published 2021 by Good2Go Publishing
7311 W. Glass Lane • Laveen, AZ 85339
www.good2gopublishing.com
https://twitter.com/good2gobooks
G2G@good2gopublishing.com
www.facebook.com/good2gopublishing
www.instagram.com/good2gopublishing

Love, is a gift that two hearts will appreciate unwrapping. Find your true heart and unwrap your happiness.

—Warren C. Holloway

ONE

Sometimes we chase after a life of love that isn't meant for is. The boys, the men with their games, lies, cheating, and deceit. Some of us even gravitate toward those type of boys and men. Why? Because we seek comfort in them, not realizing that if we love ourselves first, then we will find a love that mirrors that emotion we have inside of us. My name is Angel Renee Waters, and this is my story of me finding my true love. So follow me as I take you back to how it all started.

I was born in Southeast Washington, DC, on April 18, 1995. I had biracial parents, my mother being white, my father Afro American, working at the US Mint. However, they didn't have love for one another. She was a prostitute that gave me up for adoption. I don't hate her for her decision, since it afforded me a better life with a family in Mechanicsburg, Pennsylvania. Mrs. Shirley and Charles Estill, two caring people who have a daughter and son of their own but wanted to adopt me, adding me to the family of love. I always felt welcomed and a part of the family. Never once did I feel adopted, until was in middle school. I started realizing my biracial skin wasn't like the other white kids' at this private school. The students would ask if I had a different father than my brother Daniel and sister Caroline. I didn't know the answer at the time, so I told them they must be crazy. I later discovered I was adopted, which made me feel a little different, knowing that someone didn't love me enough to keep me. However, the Estill family wanted to love me enough to bring me into their family. Here at the Harrisburg Academy private school, I met Deborah Fisher, a slim-built model-looking girl with glowing gray eyes and perfect white teeth that stood out when she smiled, lighting up the room with her innocence. Her silky brown hair flowed down her back. She could easily be on the TV show America's Next Top Model. However she was humble in her beauty, not seeing herself as everyone else did.

I remember her approaching me in school for the first time. "Don't pay them kids any mind, questioning you about who your parents are and all. Half of them probably think their dad is their dad, when really it's their neighbor," she said, making me burst into laughter as we stood in front of my open locker, retrieving my books. "Oh, my name is Deborah Fisher. My dad owns all of the car dealerships with our last name on it, going down the Carlisle Pike," she added. Her father's dealership was the largest in Cumberland County, having cars ranging from Fords to Jaguars. "Money doesn't afford all of us manners or common sense," she said, referring to the other kids with their onslaught of questions of race and why I looked different.

"I'm Angel. Thank you for coming over and noticing me," I said, shaking her hand.

"You stand out in a good way, Angel, but not the way these uppity assholes think you do," she responded, making me smile at how forward she was. The type that always stood up to bullies. A good thing, because I tended to ignore them rather than being confrontational. From this day forward, Deborah and I became good friends, always hanging out after school, whether it was at her place in the well-to-do Pinehurst Estates, boasting million-dollar homes, or over at my parents' place in Mechanicsburg, a three thousand-square-foot bi-level, big enough to run around playing tag with Deborah and my adopted siblings. Deborah and I found this one kid in school to be very attractive: Tommy Roland, a pretty boy with his glowing blue eyes, baby face, and perfect smile with dimples. He was well dressed in the latest name brands. He also had a personal driver that brought him to school each day in his family's Rolls Royce. He got all of the girls' attention being fifteen. One would have thought he was a star. Even the girls in eleventh and twelfth grade kept vying for his attention and time. Standing five foot eleven, he had his father's genes, since his dad was six foot five.

Deborah and I both took time to write notes to him to see which one of us he would choose. It took him a day to respond, but he chose me. It was a shock to me, since I figured he would go after Deborah with her model looks. I remember staying up past my bedtime writing letters to him, so he could have them each morning when we crossed paths, since we were in different classes. The teenage puppy love stage was in full effect. The rush from the teenage crush I used to get, seeing him exit his fancy car. I would light up like a Las Vegas lightbulb, until racial slurs permeated through the air bringing me back down to the reality of where I was.

"Hey, half-breed, what are you smiling at?" a sixteen-year-old redhead yelled out, making her girlfriends point and laugh. I remember looking on at them with anger, until Tommy came over to me.

"Angel, Jay-Z said it best: Brush your shoulders off. They don't have what you have, so they're jealous," he said, leaning into kiss me on the cheek before adding, "Did you have a chance to see that movie The 6th Sense last night on TV? The end was so crazy."

"I couldn't finish watching it because it was too scary, plus I got tired writing you this note," I said, handing him the note. He smiled, appreciating my thoughtful words. At the same time the school bell sounded off, meaning we had to get to our designated classes. Right then he placed the note in his pocket before taking out a note he'd written for me. I could see the smiley face and heart on the outside of the note. I was smiling inside and out, appreciating how thoughtful he was. He even put his arm around me as we headed into the building, assuring me and those around that I was with him and they were not. The middle school puppy love transitioned to high school, where I still continued to see Tommy. Now I was sixteen and he was eighteen, readying to graduate, looking more like a male model or a future basketball star, even though he couldn't play a lick of basketball.

Tommy took me to the prom that year. His friend Joey asked Deborah out to the prom, and she came to support me, even though Joey wasn't her type. He was cute, kind, and dressed well. Deborah was more into the jocks and guys who thought they were the next big R&B singer or rapper. I was wearing a royal-blue prom dress my mother made. Tommy loved it, too, the way he kept staring at me, or maybe it was how I had filled out over the last three years. He had this look as if he wanted more tonight, he wanted to be rewarded for the long three-year wait.

Me, I was content with the kisses and just being close to him. That alone made my heart flutter. It was also enough for me to gossip with Deborah about. Deborah, on the other hand, was no longer a virgin. She allowed Ricky Barnes, the basketball team captain, to have her forbidden fruit. Then he went off to college, leaving her behind to cry in my arms, wanting him back, wishing she was a graduate to chase after him. He was her first, but didn't cherish the moment as she did. This was also the thought playing in the back of my mind, knowing that the same moment would soon come for Tommy and me, since this was also his last year.

Deborah and I found ourselves dancing together on the floor, mixing in with the crowd as the music blasted. She leaned in close to tell me something. "Are you going to give him some tonight?" Her question alone brought fear into my heart and body, because I'd never had sex. He was my boyfriend, yes, but it didn't obligate me to this, did it? I was now questioning myself, before responding to her.

"I don't want him to do what Ricky did to you, because I'll be a mess crying all over you," I said, making her facial expression change as thoughts of Ricky entered her mind, him taking her V-card.

"He's better than Ricky, plus he looks like he has a lot to offer you. If you know what I mean?" she said being funny, not realizing she was scaring me even more at the thought of something big stretching my virgin body. Not good.

"He's not worried about it, so why should I be?" I responded, being naive. What eighteen-year-old boy with his looks didn't want a beautiful female like me on prom night? The night was coming to an end. I had to be home by twelve. After the prom was the after-party. I could go there as long as the other parents were present. Some students, having celebrity or politician parents, would have their staff present to look after them.

Deborah came over hugging me goodnight. "It's okay to be scared, but enjoy yourself, it's prom night," she said, as if prom night was every teenage kids' cue to have sex, giving up their V-card. However, she was my best friend, and I valued her words and opinion. She left her date, making her way home early. She'd probably try to reach out to Ricky, since prom night was when she lost her precious fruit last year.

We headed out into the S600 Mercedes Benz limo Tommy's father rented for us. Inside of it was just as nice as the Rolls Royce they had. "Did you have fun tonight, Angel Renee?" Tommy asked, making my name sound so sweet and romantic.

"Yes, I had fun dancing with you and my crazy best friend," I said, thinking about her words. I could feel the limo driving off. The interior lights dim, and the minibar lights displayed the bottles of liquor and champagne—something most companies would have removed, knowing they were doing a prom run. Tommy, being spoiled, had his ways of getting what he wanted. He took hold of a bottle of Grey Goose vodka. It was a very pretty bottle, I thought as he grabbed two glasses as if he'd done this before. Maybe he practiced?

"One for you, and one for me," he said, handing me a double shot. I didn't drink or smoke, and he knew this. However, I was holding the glass, not resisting it. "This is just for the night. I know it's not your thing, but what better way to end the night than to share a drink with the world's most beautiful female with those sparkling eyes and smile?" he said, dressing his approach up.

We drank the shots. The vodka seemed to be hot,

burning as it went down my throat. He took my glass and placed it on the bar, where he retrieved a Hershey's Kiss. "Eat this. It'll make your tongue feel a little better from the stinging of the alcohol," he said unwrapping the chocolate and placing it to my lips, before I opened my mouth and ate it. A smile graced his face, feeling the buzz from the double shot. At the same time the chocolate started to melt over my tongue, the alcohol also hit me. This buzzing feeling was good. He leaned in to kiss me. I didn't resist because I enjoyed his lips on mine. However, being buzzed was making this kiss even more exciting, with emotions to it. His hands were starting to come into play, touching my leg, slowly making its way up into my inner thigh. My heart was starting to beat fast feeling his hand closing in on my place of passion. Then he paused, using his free hand to unbutton his pants. Now both hands were in play, one on my leg sliding up my dress, the other touching my breast. The feeling of butterflies backed by the buzz I was feeling was stimulating emotionally and physically. His fingers parted my panties to the side. I jerked back slightly, and he paused briefly, only to resume, slowly finding me, caressing my close-shaven area, before sliding his fingers across and parting all of me. My breathing was picking up, feeling the thickness of his single finger entering. I squirmed, at the same time letting out a light moan. "Aaaah." This never-before-feeling was a first. As strange as it may sound, I never even had mastu-rbated, so his touch was stirring something up inside of me. The fear I had of sex was being overshadowed by a sensation of butterflies bouncing around inside of my body. The alcohol added to this situation. His finger made my body heated yet ready and wet for him. His finger came to a slow halt. My panties were now coming off, sliding over my legs. Then my dress was being pulled up, exposing my flesh. He rubbed his stiffness up against my sacred place, which was about to be shared with him. I could feel the pressure of his thickness entering, filling me up.

"Mmmmmhh, ooooh, it's tight," I let out as he pressed deep into my body. His motion ignited another feeling I never experienced before. This feeling was also making my heart flutter with passion as his lips found my neck. A part of me was thinking, "How could I have feared something that feels so good?" The other part of me, knew what I was doing

16

was supposed to be shared with someone special, with the one guy I loved and cared about. Tommy Roland was that guy. Suddenly bringing me back into the moment, an orgasmic wave streamed through my body. I could feel my stomach tightening, my legs shaking, my breathing picking up as moans filtered into the limo. "Mmmmmmh, mmmmmmmmh, what's happening? Mmmmmh, oooooooh my," I said unaware that this powerful orgasm I was having was a part of sex.

This feeling I had this very moment for the first time was so good, and it was magnifying my feelings for him. This uncontrollable pulsating feeling was rushing from my body, escaping along with the moans. "Aaaaah, mmmmmmh, aaaaaah." His pace was now picking up, adding to the intense pleasure.

Then it happened: this eruption from him into my body, triggering a feeling inside of me, making me release even more. His motion was coming to a slow, his kisses covered my face and lips, making me feel appreciated, as if I did the right thing in choosing the right guy to share my virginity with.

"I love you, Tommy. Thank you for being nice to me and waiting three years," I said, looking into his eyes and feeling on top of the world as a young teen. He removed himself from me, pulling his pants back up, before sliding my panties on me. We kissed and smiled, looking into each other's eyes.

"I love you too. I wish you could come to college with me, but no matter where I am, I'll be thinking of you," he said, leaning in and placing another kiss to my lips. Right in this moment I knew I did the right thing in sharing this time with him. "Now I have to get you home before your parents kill me and I won't make it to college," he said, making me laugh.

"I'll stop them before that happens. I would lie down in front of them, giving you enough time to run," I said, adding to our laughter and good time. His hand was now gently rubbing my leg as he was looking into my eyes. I wanted more of this new thing, the feeling he just gave me, making my heart, mind, and body come alive. I placed my hand on his lap.

He looked at me as if he knew what I wanted. "We'll have plenty of time in our future for this. Trust me, each time will be more special than the last as we chase this great feeling," he said taking his hand and running it through my hair before kissing my forehead, as if to mark his queen. "You're the one, Angel Renee. I told my parents this when we first met. Now look at us a few years later. I still see you as if it's the first time I set eyes on you." His words were mature, yet making me feel good.

I leaned in, caressing his neck, looking into his eyes, appreciating him. "We don't have to miss each other when you go to college. We can write or talk every night," I said as the limo came to a halt. I looked out the window seeing we were at my house. My father was standing in the doorway looking at his watch. It was cutting it close, but we were on time. I started fixing myself up, not wanting to look disheveled like we were doing things a father wouldn't approve of.

"Take this mint, so he doesn't smell the vodka,"

Tommy said, thinking smart. He also popped one in his mouth as the chauffeur came and opened the door. We exited, looking as we did when we left.

My father smiled as we approached, proud that Tommy honored his curfew. "I like you, young man. You brought my baby girl home safe. I hope you were respectful to her too?"

"Yes, sir, she's a lady and wouldn't have it any other way," Tommy responded. It made me smile, appreciating his response.

"Well, say goodbye, young man."

"As my parents always say, it's never goodbye, it's I'll see you later," he responded. "I'll see you later, beautiful. I enjoyed this memorable prom night," he said, embracing me with a hug knowing my father wouldn't approve of him kissing me.

"Thank you for being nice to me and everything I could ever want this night to be," I whispered into his ear. We parted from the hug, and he made his way back to the car, standing at the door watching me enter the house with my father.

Once inside of the house, I ran up to my room to text Deborah.

Angel: OMG I did it!!!
Deborah: Really???
Angel: U didn't tell me it was going to be good. It was so special. Before and afterward.
Deborah: Before like tongue before or tongue after before?
Angel: What?? I didn't understand the oral sex reference at the time, since the sex thing was all new to me.
Deborah: Condom or the real deal?

Oh my God, now that she asked me this, I didn't even think about it. Now my mind was racing as my heart was pounding, thinking, "What if I get pregnant?"

Angel: It was all too real, but a very good, never-before feeling. I wanted to do it again, but we pulled up to the house.

Deborah: UR a freak already, LOL.

Angel: I'm not a freak, crazy. Just found this new feeling that makes me happy.

Deborah: That feeling's name is Tommy. LOL.

Deborah: Glad you had fun and he made the night special for you. I had fun, too, then came home. Wasn't feeling the selection of guys.

What she really meant was she didn't want to think about how Ricky did her on this very night last year. But she was my best friends, so I didn't hassle her about it.

Angel: More details in the AM. Got to shower

and sleep. Luv ya. I showered before finding myself

in bed, holding the pillow, flashing back to the limo,

until I went to sleep with a smile on my heart and

face.

TWO

The next day, Saturday morning, I was awakened by Deborah sitting at my bedside staring back at me, throwing stuffed animals at me to wake me up. When I zoomed in on her face, she was shaking her head with a smile.

"What's all of this about?" I asked, sitting up in my bed.

"You were sleeping with a mile-wide grin on your face. I take it you couldn't stop thinking about last night?"

She was right. What else could I think about? "Like you never thought about Ricky afterward."

"I still do, but he's an asshole for forgetting about me as if what we did wasn't special." Most girls rush to give themselves, like my best friend, not realizing Ricky had her lined up along with other girls, something she discovered through social media.

"How did you get in, Deborah?"

"Daniel. You know he has a thing for me. He's waiting until I turn eighteen, with him being nineteen. Not that it matters to me, but he doesn't want your dad to kill him. Anyway, you want to grab some breakfast at the diner or takeout?" Her tone of voice let me know she wanted to talk about something else that was bothering her.

"Let me get myself together," I said, getting out of the bed and making my way to the bathroom.

"Is everything okay, Deborah?" I asked.

"If not, it will be," she responded, which made me anxious to know what was going on with my best friend.

I hurried to freshen up. I was ready within thirty minutes. "I think the diner would be good. We can get a booth to have our morning gossip," I said as we exited the house.

Deborah only had a permit, but her father still gave her a car with dealer tags to drive. His princess got whatever she wanted. A CL55 AMG Mercedes Benz was today's choice. I always enjoyed riding with her in different cars every week, and sometimes she would switch during the week. We headed to the diner in Harrisburg on Herr Street. I liked this diner because although it was in the city, the hospitality was nice. Deborah and I stood out from the normal customers in the city.

We found our corner booth and ordered the food.

Then the conversation of what was wrong came into play.

"So what brings you and I to this place outside of breakfast?" I asked.

"I heard my parents arguing last night and then this morning. I mean it's probably nothing, but I never heard my father get that loud or my mother seem so angry. It scared me to think that he may have hurt her, or she may have brought pain to him. I even started thinking with their arguing, they could be thinking of divorce or something." She paused, taking a breath, at the same time processing her thoughts on every scenario. Her thoughts made her emotional. I could see it in her eyes.

"No one wants their parents to separate or be mad at one another. I don't want to come from a broken home," she added, sounding spoiled, pouring her heart out. "I don't want to be without either of my parents." The waitress came over and placed our milk and orange juice in front of us.

"Thank you," I said before she walked away. "Deborah, instead of assuming what the problem is, you should ask your parents why they were arguing. You are their daughter and have the right to know, especially if it affects you," I said, then took a drink of the orange juice.

"Thank you for your feedback, Dr. Waters," she said, being funny, yet able to smile, which was good. "I don't like seeing my BF or anyone being down. Now onto how your night was, details."

"Just like that, huh? It started with the vodka he had. That stuff works fast," I said, smiling. "He was gentle, his touch, from his fingertips to his lips. I melted into him. The fear of my first time faded with each pulsating wave of pleasure strung by his touch."

"Okay, okay, stop right there. The way you're describing it is so vivid, I almost felt like I was there and he was touching me," she said with a smile, making me laugh. "I am really happy for you, Angel. I think he's the type you can marry and be your high school sweetheart." Hearing her say this made me feel good, knowing I made the right decision in sharing my greatest gift with him, my body.

Interrupting our conversation, the food came. I ordered bacon, scrambled eggs with cheese and onions, and a toasted bagel. Deborah ordered the New York strip steak with fried eggs on the side, hash browns, and toast.

"This food is good. I need this every day," she said, cutting a piece of the steak and passing a piece over to me. "It's seasoned just right. Taste it," she added.

I obliged, taking a bite of the steak, which melted on my tongue. I looked over by the kitchen giving the cook a thumbs-up. He nodded his head, thankful that his food was being appreciated.

"Deborah, when was the last time you saw someone outside of Ricky?"

She paused from her food, taking a drink of her juice to chase the food down. "Being honest, he was my first and last. Even if you think I use other guys to get over him, they never get what he got, because I waited thinking he would come back." Hearing her say this was a surprise since she flirted with guys quite often. Maybe she was feeling them all out to see what they really wanted from her. The other part of my mind was wondering how she could go from that night to nothing else. Maybe her night wasn't like mine with Tommy.

"I'm not judging you, but I would have driven to his college and made him give me some. Then I would have kicked his ass afterward for making me drive so far," I said, being truthful and funny at the same time.

"It's his loss, especially if I get this modeling gig."

"What modeling gig?" I asked, shocked to hear this for the first time.

"My dad paid this professional to take pictures of me, then sent them to IMG in New York."

"My good friend is going to become the next Gisele in her Victoria's Secret fashion show, leaving me behind, in little old Mechanicsburg," I said, making her laugh.

"I'll take you with me because you're beautiful and different and they like different."

"I'm five foot two. That's too short," I responded.

"Not with six-inch red bottoms on," she stated.

"You're the model, Deborah, and you'll be the best ever, making Ricky kick his own ass for turning his back on you."

Before she was able to respond, the door opened and chimed, getting her attention, seeing two black males entering. The first stood five foot ten and was in shape with his Jordan 23 jersey on displaying his muscular frame. He had Ray-Ban shades on, looking like a rapper with his close cut on top, faded on the side, with a platinum chain on boasting a diamond-encrusted cross. The other male was six-foot-two with darker skin than the other. He was medium built and also in shape, with a baby face and curly hair and Gucci glasses flowing with his Gucci watch and loafers that complemented the jeans and white tank top.

"Look at these two coming in looking like Jeezy and Skin," Deborah said with a smile. They also noticed Deborah and I, since we stood out, being the lighter and whiter of the customers. They found a seat not too far from ours. The tall one focused on his order and food while the other kept cutting his eye over at us.

"I think he's checking you out Deborah since you're the model," I said, wanting to direct her attention to him, since this was not the type she went after. I wanted her to try someone different, not the guys she normally thought highly of.

"He is cute and flashy with his bling and biceps on display," she said.

The waitress came over and gave us the check. Deborah was paying for it, since she had the bank card from her dad, which gave her an allowance larger than most adults' checks.

As we were preparing to leave, the brown-skinned one with the jersey on spoke up. "You two beautiful ladies is just going to leave without introducing yourself?" he said, standing from his seat and making eye contact with Deborah then me before going back to her.

"I'm sixteen. My name is Angel, and my best friend is the same age. Her name is Deborah. She's going to be a model," I said, proud and happy for her.

"I'm not going to be a model just yet."

"Because you already are, from what I see," he responded quickly but smoothly. "My name is Shane, and this is my big brother, Ivan Jr. So we going to exchange numbers, or y'all too good for that?" he said, being forward.

Deborah gravitated to his directness, reaching out and touching his bicep. "Let me see your phone," she said, entering her number into his phone. Then she asked. "How old are you?"

"Eighteen, is that too old for you?"

"I doubt my parents would have a problem with

that," she said, then added, "I never talked to a black guy before, but you are hot, and you look like a rapper."

"Why did she just say that?" I was thinking. That was way too much for a first impression. He didn't care; he just laughed it off.

"I'll hit you up later to see what you doing," he said before looking over at me. "You can give my big bro your number."

"I doubt it. I have someone, but your brother is sexy," I said, turning to head over with Deborah to pay the bill before exiting. Once outside I let Deborah know she was extra with the black guy thing. "You know a guy doesn't need to know if you ever dated outside of your race in the first seconds of meeting him."

"I don't think it bothered him. He probably knows a lot of white girls that want him because he looks good and famous," she said as we were getting into the car.

My cell phone sounded off. I glanced down and saw it was Tommy. My heart was feeling his presence as I answered the call with excitement. "Hi, Tommy."

"Hello, beautiful, you sound alive and well," he responded, hearing my tone of voice.

"I am alive and well thanks to you being a gentleman, making me feel like a young queen with your royal treatment," I said, making him feel good.

"I want to see you sometime today, if it is possible. We can go to a movie or dinner, whatever you like."

"Deborah and I just finished eating breakfast. We can have a late lunch then a movie," I said, wanting just to be close to him, sharing his space, and maybe a repeat.

"You have my girl whipped already, Tommy!" Deborah yelled out, embarrassing me. I tried to cover the phone, but he heard her.

"Someone sounds a little left out," he stated.

"She's okay. She just met someone that will have her attention if he's nice to her," I said. She was shaking her head, not wanting me to mention him until she figured him out. "I'm on my way home. I'll be there gossiping with Deborah about the latest."

"Really?" he responded, knowing I would inform my best friend of the details. I couldn't keep my first time from my best friend. "Everything isn't meant to be shared with friends," he said, being a little more conservative.

"When good things happen to me or in my life, I want the world to know, or at least my best friend."

"I guess it's a female thing. However, when good things do happen, it was meant to be," he said, making me feel even better about him. "How about sushi? There's a real nice place called Saburo's on Carlisle Pike. They serve some of the best Japanese cuisine. My parents took me there a few times."

"I'll try it. I hope you know what to get me, so I'm not grossed out," I said.

"New things, beautiful. Open your mind to new things, and you'll see the world and everything around you in a different light," he said, not realizing he had planted a mental note in my head to be open-minded.

"I'm open to giving you my heart, mind, and body, so that is a start. The rest we'll take slow, one thing and one day at a time, okay? I'll see you later."

"I can't wait," he replied before hanging up the phone. As always since we met three years ago, he placed a smile on my heart and face.

"I'm really happy for you two. I can't wait until I'm where you are with him, so we can double date," Deborah said.

"If that rapper look-alike doesn't stick around treating you right, then when you become a super-model, every guy in the world will chase behind you, to take you out and spoil you."

"Yeah, fat old rich guys," she said, laughing at the image.

She pulled up to my house feeling better than she did when she came over. "Text me with all of the goods of your day with Tommy, your future hubby, no details left out," Deborah said.

"The same goes for the rapper look-alike when he calls you. Tell me if he's worth holding onto," I said, then shifted back to the serious topic. "Have that talk with your parents. It's important they know how you feel about them arguing," I said before waving as she drove off.

I made my way into the house, where my brother Daniel was staring out of the window, since he had a thing for Deborah. "So when is Deborah's birthday, Angel?" my brother asked.

"Nevuary thirty second. She's not for you, Daniel."

"How could you say that, knowing I'm a good person?"

"Because it would be weird if you and her didn't work out. My brother dating my best friend."

Yeah that wouldn't be cool, especially the way she was outspoken. She would want to give details that would be repulsive to me. Then if they didn't work, I would feel awkward having her come around, so that was a negative. I headed up the stairs to get ready for my day with Tommy, smiling in the process, reflecting back to last night and looking for more of that feeling that took me, my body, and my heart by storm.

THREE

Tommy's car pulled up to the front of my house. At the same time I received a text message from him making me aware of this. I made my way out to him. He stood outside of the Rolls Royce in his two-piece white linen, tailored to his fit frame, looking very comfortable with his Sean Jean loafers.

"You always look amazing, Angel Renee," he said as I approached him with a smile, hoping he would like what I was wearing since I changed outfits a few times. The blue D&G jeans fit perfectly, showing my developing curves. My powder-blue D&G top was snug, and I wore the three-inch heels my father didn't care for, as he said they made me look older. I don't know how, but he had a protective eye.

"You look sexy, too, with your innocent smile that is not so innocent," I said, referring to last night. He gave me a hug before allowing me to get into the backseat. Once the door closed and our conversation started, the driver took off heading to our lunch destination.

"These flowers are for you, beautiful," he said, taking hold of the flowers that were lying in between the front seats. "I want you always to feel special when I'm around, or even when you're thinking of me," he added as I took hold of the roses, smelling them.

"Thank you for the roses and being thoughtful,"

I said, removing the roses from my nose to lean in and kiss him on the cheek. Then he turned to face me, so another kiss followed. My lips locking with his made me feel good inside and out. "Thank you, baby," I said again after the kiss. This thanks was more for how he made me feel when we kissed.

"So I looked up sushi online since I never had it. I saw some things I wouldn't mind trying for the first time," I said. He gave me this look with a smile, appreciating the time I took to look it up. "Tokyo Sunrise with quail eggs and caviar on the top. It also looks pretty."

"Funny you mentioned that one. It's my favorite. Each bite seems to burst with flavor. I like that you're willing to try new things."

"New relationship, new love, new start equals all

new things we can share together," I said, placing a smile on his face.

"I like the sound of this," he said, placing a kiss on my lips. "Does this mean we can start this day off like it's our first time?" he added, referring to being intimate with me last night. It was turning me on how his lips touched my ear when he whispered to me, accompanied with images of last night.

"We'll see how lunch and the movie turn out."

"Sushi then a movie at my place, since my parents are gone until tomorrow."

Hearing him say this, I knew how this date was going to end. At least how he and I anticipated it ending. These were my true thoughts as a young sixteen-year-old girl in love with her boyfriend of three years. Most adult couples don't even stay together that long.

The car pulled up to the sushi restaurant, and we exited looking like Hollywood's young elite. Like a gentleman, he held the door as we entered the restaurant.

"It looks really nice in here, like we left America and entered Japan," I said, taking in all of the Asian decor.

"Table for two, follow me, please," the server said. We followed her over to a table in the center of the room. Right then I was feeling the spotlight on us, having to sit in the middle. Some of the people present, along with the staff, knew Tommy and his family and waved to him. He pulled my chair out before sitting across from me. I could see the love in his eyes.

"I hope this thing we have lasts forever, like my parents who met in high school," he said. This alone allowed me to know this was where he got his guidance from. He, like most children, looked up to and aspired to be like their parents. He'd been taught well how to treat a female. He'd also learned from his mother how a woman wants to be treated. I'm thankful to his parents for him.

"You make me happy, Tommy. My heart literally flutters when you're around, or when I know I'm going to be seeing you. Maybe it's a teenage crush thing or puppy love. Either way, I'm enjoying every second of it," I said, smiling and looking on at him with affection.

"You're the one, Angel Renee, and whether it's puppy love or a teenage crush, we'll grow it into something stronger, more noticeable and powerful, that will make us gravitate toward it each day." Hearing his words made me place my hand over my beating heart, as if he was whispering these words to my heart and touching it emotionally.

"I love you too," I said. We placed our order, the food came, and we talked more about him going off to college and our future while he was at Harvard. The line of communication was important in a long-distance relationship.

After sushi we made our way out to watch a movie at his parents' mansion located in New Cumberland, called the Cliffs. All the homes boasted four- and five-car garages, each well over ten thousand square feet, some with custom fountains in front for decor. This was my first time at his place.

We always met elsewhere. Even when I met his parents, it was at functions, since they were always traveling for business. Now that I was coming here, it made this thing we had even more official.

"Welcome to my home, which may be our place one day, when my parents decide to downgrade to something smaller." When he said "our home," it made me gravitate toward him, placing a kiss on his lips, because he was thinking far into the future.

"Follow me to the entertainment area," he said taking me to the elevator. This was also impressive. I could get used to this, I was thinking, holding onto his arm as the elevator went down.

"This house could be on TV, like the rappers and celebrities showing off their mansions," I said, making him smile.

"This is all for comfort, not for showing off," he said. As the doors opened, he took my hand, leading me to the large home theater. As we entered, the lights came on low, detected by our movement. He took the remote that was on the plush dark red leather love seat. "Action, romance, or drama?" he asked.

"Action, since we're living our own romance together," I said, smiling yet making him laugh. He selected Training Day featuring Denzel. "Is it too early in the day for some of that stuff you gave me last night?" I asked, wanting to be as it was before, setting the mood. It was crazy because before last night, drinking wasn't my thing, but I liked that feeling and how it all played.

"Take a seat, and I'll see what I can find for the lady." I sat down on the plush love seat, almost sinking in it. It didn't take long before he returned with a bottle of Patrón Silver, it read on the outside of the bottle. He filled two glasses, more than I had last night. "This is tequila. It's a little different than last night, but it's just as good," he said, handing me a full glass. "A toast to our promising future together and me doing good at Harvard."

"To our young but growing love," I said, toasting his glass before drinking half of the glass. The tequila was burning and warming at the same time. We finished the shots only to pour a little more. We drank them too. Oh my, that warm fuzzy feeling was happening. My feelings seemed to be emotionally heightened. "You know I love you, Tommy, and only you."

"You're feeling it already, huh?"

"I like the feeling of you caressing my hair," I said, looking into his eyes. He leaned in, placing a kiss to my lips. The feeling was now enhanced, like last night, but with more passion. At the same time my hand pressed up against his firm chest. His hands roamed over me, unbuttoning my top. His fingers glided over my bra down to my stomach. His touch made me flinch with pleasure, as if being caressed with a feather. Now his fingertips undid my pants, sliding and disappearing into my panties. He found me once more, strumming my pleasure with his fingers. My heart fluttered from his touch, sending a rushing sensation through my body. My moans vibrated over his tongue. As if a tease, he paused, removing his fingers from me.

"I want to do something special for you," he said,

coming out of his clothing then gracefully removing my pants and panties. "Lie back. This is going to be different but good," he said, lowering his head and body to my feet where he started kissing, then in between my thighs, until he came face-to-face with my special gift for him. His tongue closed in, unwrapping all of me, taking me and my body to a place I'd never been before.

I squirmed and moaned, clinching handfuls of his body, embracing this new powerful feeling created by the tip of his tongue and fingers, finding their way around my body as if they'd been here before. "Tommy, mmmmmmh, ooooh my, mmmmmmh," I let out, feeling this pulsating power of intense pleasure surging through my body, racing through me and creating butterflies throughout my body, making me so sensitive everywhere. My breathing was just as heavy as my moans were intense. "Aaaaah, aaaaaaah. Aaaaah, aaaaaaah. What's happening, aaaaaah, mmmmmmh," I let out, now realizing for the first time I was having multiple orgasms that were escaping my body back-to-back, flowing over his tongue and fingers that seemed to melt my heart and body, blowing my mind. A little laughter came out in between moans as I flashed back to Deborah's text message about tongue play. Now I knew what she meant, and it felt so good. I couldn't wait to tell her about this.

"Mmmmmh, mmmmmmh, my body loves this feeling," I moaned, being taken with each pulsating lash of his tongue and stroking fingers. He paused, looking up at me. I didn't want him to stop. He came up kissing me as he took his length and thickness and pressed it into my body, creating another wave of orgasmic pleasure. "Aaaaaah, aaaah, aaaaaah, baby, baby, mmmmmmh, mmmmmmh." Lost in this moment of passion, I didn't want him to leave for college. I wanted every day to be like this, I was thinking as his flow rushed into me. We continued on having fun because I liked the thing he was doing with his tongue and fingers together. After the fun, we did watch the movie before we passed out from the session and alcohol.

9:23 PM

I opened my eyes not realizing how long I'd been sleep or what time it was, until I heard my cell phone chiming, making me aware I had missed multiple calls and texts. Calls and text from Deborah.

Deborah: 8:34 PM Where R U???
Deborah: 9:01 PM U R dad called me. He wants to
know where U R.

Reading the texts sobered me up by the second. I

didn't mean to worry my dad.

"Tommy, get up," I said, nudging him to wake

up. He opened his eyes and saw my face and knew

something was wrong.

"Oh my God, how long have I been asleep?" he

asked, sitting up, not wanting to be on my dad's bad

side.

"We have to go. Deborah said my dad was look-

ing for me."

He jumped up, placing his clothes on. I did the

same. He handed me some Altoids to get rid of the

smell of alcohol from my breath.

Angel: I'm w/Tommy on my way home.
Deborah: He better have made it worth you getting

in trouble!
Angel: Details in the AM if I survive my dad LOL
Deborah: Luv U, goodnite

Tommy's driver took me home. Tommy came with, but he stayed in the car so he wouldn't have to explain himself to my father. I exited the car fast, seeing my dad stepping off the porch.

The car drove off as my father started to speak. "You have some explaining to do, young lady. How can you go all day without telling me and your mother where you were going? Then to top it off you don't answer the phone. Your mother is in there worried half to death." I was in the wrong, but being with Tommy made me feel so right. I had to blame it on the alcohol, because we blacked out. I never would have not answered my parents' calls.

"I'm sorry, Dad, I didn't realize my phone was

off, and, yes, I should have told you where I was going. I did tell Daniel to let you know where I was going." I didn't tell my brother anything, but as his little sister, he would cover for me. Besides, he was still keeping his hopes alive for dating Deborah.

"Your brother is going to have to answer to me for not telling me where you were," my father stated, shifting his attention from me to him. I took advantage and walked past him quickly before he could smell the alcohol, because there would be no explaining that away. I would be grounded for a month of Sundays. I ran up to my bedroom and sprayed perfume on, followed by gargling mouth-wash, before going to my mother's room. I made her aware of the phone story and me relaying info to my brother. She didn't seem as upset as my father said.

She was happy to see that I was okay though. After the brief talk I dashed back to my room and brushed my teeth and then showered to get rid of the traces of evidence of my day that would make me the center of attention again. Then I jumped in bed, thanking God for the day, for my boyfriend, and for not allowing me to get into trouble with my parents. Then I fell asleep thinking about my future husband, Tommy Roland.

FOUR

Sunday morning came, and as always I got up with the rest of the house to go to church. The entire time I was there, I was thinking about Tommy Roland. "God forgive me for having sinful thoughts of last night while I'm in your house," I was thinking. After church we shared a family dinner at around four in the evening. After dinner I reached out to Deborah via text.

Angel: Come over
Deborah: w/rapper look-alike
Angel: Already???
Deborah: Not like that, not saying it won't be. It has been awhile.
Angel: Details about last night when U R ready.
Deborah: Can't wait. I'll let you know what happens here too if anything at all.

After we finished texting, I reached out to Tommy.

Angel: Missing U already
Tommy: Still savoring dessert

His text was referring to oral passion, which took my heart, mind, and body to another place.

Angel: I luv your talents.
Tommy: U Bring that out of me, Mrs. Roland.

I read the text correctly, which further assured me he was thinking into the future. I flopped on my bed staring at the text before responding.

Angel: You really have me in UR emotional embrace.
    I feel good here in this space with you.
Tommy: You are all I need, Angel Renee.

Reading the text brought happy tears to my eyes. At the same time, I was visualizing him lying there with me, saying those thoughtful words.

Angel: U R so loving and sweeeeeet. I luv you so
    much.

I sent the message lying on my bed cuffing my

large stuffed bear, which I now called Tommy bear, because it gave me comfort.

Tommy: I have something special 4 U
Angel: Curious to know what it is. U gave me special
    yesterday LOL.
Tommy: Come out front.

Reading his text stating he was out front made me jump up and rush over to the window, where I saw the Rolls Royce. The back window came down, exposing his pretty-boy face and smile. I held my finger up for him to hold up one second. I ran into the bathroom, checking the mirror to make sure I looked good in my Sunday church flower dress. I sprayed a little Gucci Guilty perfume on before making my way downstairs, where my parents were.

"Where are you heading to, young lady?" my mother asked. "Just out front, Mom," I responded. My father stood and made his way to the window, looking through the curtains as I approached the car. Tommy exited, standing outside of the car with his arms open to welcome me into his embrace.

"I like that you came over here to surprise me," I said.

"I have another surprise for you," he responded, removing a jewelry box from Kings Jeweler from his pocked. He opened it, revealing a necklace with a heart-shaped pendant encrusted with our initials.

"This is so beautiful with our initials inside the heart," I said, wanting and ready to kiss him, until he made me aware my father was still in the window.

"He's still looking at us," Tommy said, taking the necklace out of the box. "Let me put it on you."

I turned around and looked over at my father, who was smiling, seeing Tommy doing this. More points for Tommy, being a respectful young man. If only he knew about the last two nights, he would be chasing Tommy around with his shotgun. I turned back around and hugged him with the love and affection he was pouring on me. What more could I ask for?

"I want to always make you and your heart smile, Angel Renee. When I head off to college, this pendant is a reminder that my heart will always be with you." My eyes watered, warmed by the love and affection. "This feeling we have right now for one another is just the beginning of a good thing. Can you see that far into our future of love?" he asked, catching me by surprise since I was smitten by his every soothing word.

"I see a happy family with you, and two kids."

"A boy and a girl," he added, smiling.

"The perfect family. We'll have a princess and a young prince to love and spoil," I said. His eyes veered to the right, checking to see if my father was no longer in the window. Me noticing him earlier probably made him get away from it to leave us be. I raised up on my toes and kissed him, until we both heard the front door of the house shut. I turned around in fear that my father as going to be upset, only to see it was my brother Daniel.

"What's up, Tommy? You should think about asking my parents to rent you a room in the house instead of standing out here," Daniel said, making his way over to his Toyota Camry. I stuck my tongue out at my brother, ignoring him, yet glad it wasn't my father coming through the door.

"Your brother never has a sense of humor. Normally he's staring me down."

"He knows you're serious about me and not out for one thing like most boys."

"I did come around for one thing, you, your heart, and your soft body," he said, being funny yet making me smile.

"That's three things, silly."

"You're all I need in one," he added, placing another kiss to my lips. "I'm going to go. I have to go somewhere with my parents. They want to spend a lot of time with me since I'm going to college soon. My mother cries every time we go shopping for things I'll need there."

"I'll cry, too, when you leave," I said, leaning into his embrace. "Call or text me when you're done with your parents."

"I look forward to it, beautiful," he said, kissing my forehead before getting into the car and driving off. As soon as I entered the house, I showed my parents the necklace. "Look at what Tommy gave me."

"This is beautiful, darling," my mother said. "That boy is a keeper. He reminds me of your father when we were your age. He used to pop up with flowers, gifts, love letters, some I still have til this day." Hearing my mother say this made me realize even more that Tommy was the one.

"God sent you a blessing in that young man. Just as he did with sending your mother into my life," my father said.

"Charles, you're so sweet, darling," my mom

said, looking on at him with love. This was what I wanted for Tommy and me.

"I guess I'll leave you two love birds to reflect on good memories while I head up to my room," I said, giving each of them a kiss on the cheek before vanishing up the steps.

9:07 PM

I was watching TV when a text came through from Deborah.

Deborah: OMG! OMG! OMG!

Reading this made me so curious and slightly scared at the same time, wondering what was making her so excited like this.

Angel: What???
Deborah: I did it. Don't judge me. Right then I knew what and whom she was talking about.
Angel: Okay, I'm all ears #Details
Deborah: Sneaking in.

Her last response meant she was coming into my house through my bedroom window, by the tree she climbed to get to the roof. It didn't take long before she got to the house, making her way in through the window. I came over, hugging her.

"What are you wearing, Angel?" she questioned.

"Tommy's Harvard T-shirt with a pair of his silk boxer shorts," I responded, wrapped in the image of him and me. "Now get to the goods before my parents come checking on me, wondering how you got in here."

She jumped on my bed, lying on her back with her eyes closed as she began to talk. "He is what they say about black guys down there. Anyway, we went to dinner, then a movie, but before the movie he smoked a blunt. I never had it, so I wanted to try it.

He didn't let me, but he did pull out these pretty pink pills with a stamp of a lady on them. He called it ecstasy. He said it enhances your mood and said I would see the movie different." She paused, caressing my sheets on the bed as if it was all new to her. "This feeling from the pills makes your body so sensitive, I was touching him in the theater feeling his hard body come alive. Then he touched me." Her breathing seemed to pick up the more she was describing what took place. "His touch glided over my body, my hand on his guiding him to where I wanted to be pleased. I didn't care if people in the theater were watching."

"Oh my God, you didn't do it in the theater?"

"That's where we got started, mmh," she responded, thinking about his touch. "We rushed out to his Yukon Denali. He drank Hennessey from the bottle before passing it to me. It added to the feeling," she said opening her eyes and smiling, still high from the pills, taking her hand over her own body. "Once we were naked I reached down and felt all of him extending from my grasp. My heart started thumping, never having something this big, bigger than Ricky. I told him to be nice. He took my legs over my shoulders, and then you know what happened next. This magnified feeling from the pretty pink pills took over my body and mind," Deborah said, now with her hand partially in her pants.

I took hold of my heart-shaped pillow and tossed it at her face, making her open her eyes to reality. "What are you doing, crazy?" I asked.

She didn't even realize her hand was in her pants

until my eyes directed her to what she was doing. Right then she removed her hand quickly, feeling embarrassed. "I should go home now. He got me twisted."

"No, the pills you took have you twisted. Now sit up and focus."

"Okay, okay, best friend who is acting like my mom," she responded, laughing at her own words. "He stretched my little body out in the backseat. I think he's a freak."

"That would make you a freak, too, since he wasn't in the backseat by himself," I said, making her laugh even more.

"But I'm a good girl freak."

"Whatever, continue the story."

"He had me open, and I let him in the back door.

It was like being a virgin all over again. My body reacted to everything he did to me, making me literally slide across the backseat I was so turned on."

I started laughing at her craziness, being high from the pills and new boyfriend. "You gave him the goodies, so he better be nice to you outside of the backseat life, because you want him to also respect you."

"We're going to Hershey Park this weekend. My sweet chocolate rapper look-alike is taking me to his chocolate world." We both laughed before I filled her in on my time with Tommy. We didn't keep secrets or details from each other. That's what made us good friends.

FIVE

Three months later the summer months were coming to an end. It was the best summer, especially since I shared most of it bonding with Tommy Roland. Deborah also continued her relationship with Shane. Her detailed stories became funnier each time. Shane always encouraged her to pursue her modeling. He even drove her up to New York for her first photo shoot after IMG picked her up. She sent me pics and tweets each time. She wasn't too busy to celebrate her seventeenth birthday in June.

Today she and I were over at the Macy's in Camp Hill, not too far from where I live.

"Angel, come over here. I want to show you this

dress." I came over to her. "What do you think about it?" she asked.

I didn't think much of it at first. "It's fashionable, something you would wear," I responded.

"You don't see anything else about this that stands out?"

"Is she pregnant?" I was thinking, knowing when she got like this she had something up her sleeve. I looked at the dress then around her. That's when I noticed the large poster off to the side with her and a few other male and female models posing for YSL. "OMG! This is crazy. Look, everybody, my best friend is a model on this poster!" I blurted out in excitement before hugging her. "You made it Deborah," I said, pulling back from the hug. "Don't get all Hollywood on me either."

"I would never get too busy for family or friends. That is a sexy picture, huh?"

"Guys in school will have this all over their bedrooms, maybe in their lockers too," I said, humored by the image.

"Take a selfie of us standing here by the poster, Angel." I did just that with a big smile. "Send it to my phone, so I can forward it to Shane to see his reaction."

"I hope he doesn't become jealous of your success and the attention you'll get." Shane sent her a text in response to the picture she just sent him.

Shane: I'm the luckiest man in my city.

"Tell him he's the luckiest man in the world, because he has you, a soon-to-be supermodel."

She did just that, sending him a message.

Shane: I was the luckiest man in the world the day we met.

His response even better than I expected it to be. It also made her light up.

"I think I love him already," she said, holding onto the words of his message. She also appreciated him for being a part of her dream and pushing her to chase after it.

Deborah: I love you, Shane.
Shane: It's the world's greatest feeling. I luv U2.

I read the text, seeing the two of them were in a good space, which made me feel good that she'd found her happy place. "You have a good thing with him. Now you have to balance the two."

"What two?"

"Modeling and a relationship, since you love the two."

"Whatever happens is meant to be, my father always says."

Suddenly shifting my attention, I started feeling sick. I only ate a soft pretzel with mustard, which I chased down with a strawberry slushy.

"What's wrong with you? You have to take a dump in the middle of Macy's?" Deborah asked, smiling.

"I think my stomach is upset from the pretzel I ate."

"We can sue them if you get sick. Then you can own that pretzel stand."

"It's not that serious," I said as the feeling dissipated.

"So when is your next modeling gig?"

"The fall fashion show in New York, if my

parents let me, since it may interfere with school."

"I hope they do so you can get your big break in the business." She could do a tutor or at-home schooling. "There won't be any fun with you traveling the world, unless I'm with my baby Tommy." I said. At the same time, that feeling came back to my stomach. This time I also started gagging.

"That's it, I'm calling my dad so he can get the lawyer to look into this," Deborah snapped. I extended my hand, stopping her. At the same time a thought entered her mind. "Say it isn't so? Are you pregos?" she asked. My eyes widened in fear, flashing back to all of the unprotected sex with Tommy since he took my virginity. The thought of being pregnant was scaring the hell out of me, because I would not be able to explain this to my parents, who thought I was still a virgin. To top it off, how would Tommy be able to handle this, knowing he had a future going to college? So many thoughts and fears filled this moment thanks to Deborah saying it.

"Let's go to the pharmacy and get you a test right now. You can go to the bathroom and take it here," Deborah said.

We did just that, making our way to the store.

• • •

"Where do you keep the pregnancy tests?"

"Really, Deborah? You don't have to let the world know what we're looking for," I said as the gentleman pointed us in the right direction. We secured the test before heading to a bathroom.

"You want me to come in the stall with you? Do

you know how to use that thing?" Deborah asked, making me even more nervous and afraid.

"I have everything under control," I said, securing the door to the stall, at the same time praying that I was not pregnant, so I didn't have to explain to my parents. "Please, God, let me not be pregnant," I said in a low tone.

"If you're pregnant, it is God's will, you know?" Deborah said, standing on the other side of the stall leaning up against the door hearing every word I spoke.

"Say that when Shane gets you knocked up. You'll be walking the runway with your baby in hand," I said, making the two of us laugh at the image of that taking place. Then I became serious, reading over the box with the test before taking it out and doing as instructed. Then I placed it on top of the box, praying silently this time. My heart was beating. I could hear Deborah texting on her phone. I hoped she wasn't telling everybody. I waited the time needed for the results of the test, and then I opened my eyes, taking another deep breath and timidly extending my arm to reach for the test on top of the box. My hand nervously took hold of it, bringing it closer. Then I saw it: I put my head back, closing my eyes and embracing the next steps in my life. I exited the stall with mixed emotions: fear, love, and happiness all at once.

Deborah could see the test in my hand. Crazy as she was, she snatched it from me, not even caring that I urinated on it. "OMG, I'm going to be like an aunt or Godmother. Which one is better sounding?" she asked, full of excitement, not realizing my fear and confusion in this very moment. I knew that life was a precious gift, and babies were all so cute, but for adults to take care of. I didn't want to be a teen mom like I'd seen on TV. Deborah, realizing my fear, halted her chatter, but not before she snapped a picture of the test with the hashtag "Aunty Godmom coming soon." I loved my best friend, but she got out of hand at times.

"What am I going to do? How am I going to explain this to my parents?"

"Your dad may kill Tommy, so you should tell him first, before they track him."

"Be serious, please," I said, allowing her to sense my level of fear.

"Oh no, I'm sorry, Angel. Tell your parents, if

you plan on keeping the baby, which I think you should. Then tell Tommy because he's the father and deserves to know."

I wanted to know how far along I was, followed by how long I could keep it a secret. I didn't want my parents to look down on me or hate Tommy. "Deborah, whatever you do, don't send that pic you took."

"Too late," she said, making me even more of a wreck. "I can handle it. I'll make it seem like a prank or that it's one of the models I work with."

"Thank you. I don't want this to get out until I'm ready."

"I'll go to your appointments until you tell Tommy."

"That would be nice. Now let's get out of the

bathroom before people think we're crazy for hanging out in here," I said, thinking about the life inside of me. I could never give up on my baby, no matter how hard times got. I'd been blessed with this gift. I wondered if it was a boy or a girl. Either way, it would have plenty of love from me, Tommy, my parents, and my wild best friend.

SIX

Forty-five days later my secret was still my own. However, it was weighing on me, especially now being almost five months pregnant. Deborah managed to quiet the tweet she sent out. Tommy was doing fine in college. I missed him, although we communicated via phone, messages, and video chat. From the looks of things, my parents didn't suspect anything either. I did catch my mom giving me this look, but didn't say anything. Now I was standing in my bedroom in front of the long mirror I had on the side of my bed, with just my pajama bottoms and bra on, rubbing my growing belly. "Hello in there," I said, talking to my baby inside of me. "I love you, and soon I'm going to tell the world you're coming. You're going to be my young prince." Yes, I said prince. I was having a baby boy. No need to look for names. I already knew he was going to be a junior. "Your dad will be so excited to see you when you get here. Your crazy aunt slash Godmom is going to spoil you too," I said, having my daily talk with the life inside of me. I finally decided to tell Tommy once he got situated at college. My iPad chimed, allowing me to know that a Facetime request was coming in. I placed it on my stand so I could be hands-free for the reveal.

"Hi, babe, I miss you so much," I said, seeing his face appear. He looked happy to see me too.

"I love you, Angel Renee, and miss you just as much."

"How are things coming along there? Are the

girls throwing themselves at you yet?"

"The professors are throwing books at me. That's about it. The females here are more focused on their future of success. Not that they would be able to compete with you," he said, making me smile inside and out.

"Thank you for loving me and being so sweet. Your son will learn a lot from you on how to treat a lady," I said smoothly, revealing he was a dad. He became silent processing my words. Then it hit him. He leaned closer to the screen. "Am I going to be a dad?" he asked. I stepped back, giving him the full view of my belly.

"Your daddy wants to know if you're in there listening to us?" I said. "Yes we're pregnant. I'm five months pregos. I didn't know what to say or do. My parents don't even know. I've managed to conceal it."

"I am still taking in that I'm going to be a dad. You said a son, right? I'm going to have a little me running around." I was glad he was not upset that I kept it from him. He was so loving.

"So when will you come see us?"

"Today, since it's Friday, as long as I'm back before Monday's first class."

"I love you, and I promise to tell my parents before you get here, so they don't try to kill you," I said, hoping they were as welcoming as he was.

"Start with your mother. She'll be more understanding. Then have her break it to your father." His words comforted me. "Angel Renee, I love you. I also want to be there for every doctor's appointment if I can. Just let me know in advance."

"I have one in two weeks."

"Are you getting weird cravings yet?"

"A little bit, because I did eat some vanilla bean ice cream with pretzels."

"That sounds good. I might have to try that, sweet and crunchy."

"I had peanut butter in it too," I added.

"You may have to make that for me when I get there," he said. "Well, my love, I'm going to get ready to come see you and our growing baby boy inside of you. I love you, and I'll see you later."

"Your son and I love you even more," I said before hanging up, preparing to go speak with my parents.

My mom was in the kitchen preparing my

father's tea with skim milk and two cube sugars.

"Hi, Mom," I said, entering the kitchen. She looked over her shoulder, making eye contact with me, then back to the cup of tea. "Are you busy?" Her mother instincts kicked in, making her stop and turn around.

"I was wondering when you were going to come to me or your father," she said.

"You know?" I asked, surprised.

"I was your age once. Besides, your skin has this glow pregnant women have."

"Why didn't you say anything to me? Does dad know?"

"I'll leave that up to you to make him aware of it." There went the plan Tommy mentioned of having my mother tell him. "God doesn't make any mistakes. As much as me and your father wished you would have waited until you turned twenty-one, this is God's plan." I went over and hugged my mother, feeling this sense of relief. "How far along are you?" she asked.

"Just about five months."

"You hid this good. I hope you're eating right, for the baby's sake."

"I am. This little boy keeps me hungry," I said as my mother started rubbing my belly to greet her grandson.

"What's going on in here?" my dad asked, coming into the kitchen looking for his tea. My mother nodded her head to me to tell him.

"I love you so much, Daddy," I said, coming over to give him a hug.

"I love you too, princess. Now tell me what's going on before I get worried."

I stepped back, rubbing my belly. "I'm pregnant with your grandson."

He placed his hand over his heart, at the same time looking over at my mother. "Is this some joke you two have planned?"

"You're going to be a grandfather, Charlie," my mother said.

"I guess we're going to be babysitting while she's at school. You're not going to quit school."

"No, Dad, I know how important education is. I will graduate and go to college."

My dad crossed his arms, looking back and forth between my mother and me. "Is that Tommy Roland the father?" he asked. "If so, that boy is good. I never see him coming or going."

"I love him, Dad, and he genuinely loves me. We've known one another for a few years now. Like you two always say, you can't prevent what God wills into your life. It has already been written."

"Shirley, hand me my tea, please. I'm going to head up and pray on this," he said before kissing my cheek. Then he made his way out. I hugged my mother before leaving the kitchen to my bedroom. I sent Deborah a few texts.

Angel: Told parents about baby
Deborah: Good, no more secrets, can't wait to show you pics from fall fashion show.
Angel: I know Shane is loving it?
Deborah: It's something about that pink pill. I even felt good walking in the show, like look at me now.
Angel: Not cool Aunt 2 B
Deborah: Fun but not funny, sorry
Angel: No drugs or drama around baby

Deborah: Anything for U & baby
Angel: Tired, chat later
Deborah: You need a dose of Tommy Ro Ro to wake
    you up LOL
Angel: Soon, goodnight luv ya

I lay in bed rubbing my belly, allowing the reality

of my situation to set in. I was going to be a mother,

a good one too.

SEVEN

The morning hours seemed to come quicker than usual, especially hearing my parents moving around talking. My cell phone was chiming from the missed calls. I rubbed my belly to greet my baby.

"Good morning, baby boy, what do you want to eat today?" I said, sitting up to check my phone, seeing missed calls and messages from Deborah, Tommy, and Tommy's dad. His dad could have been calling about the baby. "Better be good things he has to say." I checked the message from Deborah first, time stamped 7:43 AM.

Deborah: I'm on my way. I hope UR okay?

"Of course I'm okay," I said knowing she was

probably still tripping from the pink pill. The next message was from Tommy.

Tommy: I really love you with all of my heart and body. I can't wait to be a family wit

His message seemed cut short, but I got what he was saying. I was his forever. I was also looking forward to his touch, rubbing my belly and even his intimate touch. Now onto Mr. Roland's text that read: "Haven't heard from my son or his driver. Is he with you?" Reading this made me nervous and worried that something was wrong. I sent messages back to everyone, before rushing into the bathroom to get freshened up.

Once I was showered and dressed, I made my way downstairs, where I immediately noticed my parents sitting around with Mr. Roland, Tommy's dad. Tears were in my mother's eyes. Right then I could feel this overwhelming feeling something was wrong.

"What's going on here?" I asked, scanning each of their faces. My mother stood and came over to me, opening her embrace. This moment I rebelled from her embrace, taking a step back. "Mom what's going on? Please tell me," I said with a shaken tone of voice. As my mom shook her head, tears filled her eyes.

"He loves you, but he's not coming." I heard my mom's words, I just didn't want to comprehend them.

"Mr. Roland please tell me Tommy is okay," I pleaded, wanting to hear different.

"He was in a car accident and he's in bad shape,"

Mr. Roland responded with his voice breaking.

"How? He has a driver."

"He wanted to surprise you early, so he left without his driver. They said he must have been texting and driving, crashing into a van killing a woman and her three kids on impact. He's currently at the Hershey Medical Center. We'll take you there as soon as you're ready," Mr. Roland said.

"I'm ready now. I want to see him," I said, crying hard, in disbelief that this was happening.

We all headed out to the cars, following Mr. Roland. My mother rubbed my back, trying to comfort and calm me.

"I know you can't help how you feel, but you don't want to stress the baby or your body," she said, still rubbing my back.

Tommy was so used to having a driver and texting, he didn't even take in to account that he couldn't drive and text all by himself.

"Leave all of your worries to God now. He has blessed you with this baby. Don't stress yourself, because I'm looking forward to being a grandmother."

Twenty plus minutes later we arrived at the Hershey trauma center. I noticed officers outside of his room, along with his mother and their family attorney. Not good.

"Honey, what's going on?" Mr. Roland asked.

"They're charging our son with vehicle manslaughter for the family in van," she responded.

My heart was heavy right now with even more bad news. Her crying was making me cry too. He couldn't go to jail. We moved passed them, entering the room. My heart ached even more seeing his bandaged and limp body in a comatose state, connected to breathing tubes in his nose and mouth. The nurse at his bedside started speaking, "He's currently in an induced coma due to the swelling of his brain, but he's young, he'll come around," she said before giving us time with him.

I started rubbing his arms and placing loving kisses on his cheek. "You better get well. We have a baby to look after," I said, wiping my tears from his face. At the same time his parents were talking about him being cuffed to the bed, my eyes shifted to his wrist. Why were they doing this?

"Mr. Roland, don't let them take him away from us," I pleaded, not wanting Tommy to go to jail.

"We have to focus on him getting better and walking out of here first. Then we will battle the legal process. Right now I want him to see your pretty face, knowing you two have a baby coming," he said, trying to cheer me up while being strong for his wife too.

Mrs. Roland came around wiping my tears and giving me a motherly hug. "We can't wait to see this baby born. Once he's better, we'll throw you a baby shower," Mrs. Roland said. I leaned over caressing Tommy's face, wanting him to get up and go home with me and the baby. I wanted him to lie next to me and rub my belly with love. I took his cuffed hand and placed it up against my belly.

"Hey, baby, it's Daddy rubbing my tummy," I said. Then I felt his hand twitch. "He just moved his fingers," I said, getting emotional and excited.

"He can hear you, keep talking," Mr. Roland said. I leaned in, allowing his hand to caress my face as I closed my eyes, flashing back to good memories far from this very moment. "Tommy, everything is going to be okay, babe. We're all waiting on you to get better. I love you just as much as our baby does," I said, standing upright and looking on at him. Then it happened again: his hand moved. "See, his hand is moving. I guess he's telling us it's going to be okay," I said.

"It's me, Tommy, your mother. Can you hear my voice? We are all waiting on you with love, so get better." His eyes blinked, making me feel even better that he was coming around, or so I thought. His eyes rolled back into his head as his body started shaking violently from the pressure on his brain, making him have a seizure. My heart leaped in fear and pain. The nurses came in fast since Mr. Roland hit the emergency button. Not realizing how overwhelmed I became, I blacked out, crashing hard to the floor. This wasn't what I envisioned our love story to be like, but we are always in God's plans.

In the darkness of my being blacked out, I saw Tommy's face, him holding our baby boy and looking on with love. Then he looked up at me. "I love you, Angel Renee. I love our baby boy too. He has your eyes and my good looks." I laughed at his words. "You didn't think I was going to leave you without telling you how much I care about you. You'll always be the one I love and hold on to. We don't say goodbye, so junior and I love you and we'll see you later," he said with love in his eyes and smile.

Suddenly the darkness became light as I opened my eyes, adjusting them to the bright lights of the hospital room. It was so bright I thought I had woken up in heaven. My parents and best friend were present, but where was Tommy? The last I remembered, I was standing at his bedside.

"Angel, I came as soon as I could," Deborah said.

"Thank you for being here," I said before shifting my attention to the doctor coming in.

"I feel good, Doc, but how is my boyfriend?" Deborah was shaking her head in a bad way. "Deborah, what's wrong?"

She looked over at my parents then back to me. "He didn't make it after the seizure." Hearing her saying this made my body tense up. At the same time

I felt like I was sinking into a dark abyss of death. "Is my baby okay?" I asked, fearing the images and statement he made in my dark black out were all too real and his way of saying goodbye, instead of see you later.

"That's what I'm here for, young lady," the doctor said. I could feel my heart thumping, my throat knotting up, my body heating up with pain. "The amount of stress on your body and the fall forced a miscarriage." He continued speaking to deaf ears as I was drowning in pain. I curled into a ball, clenching my belly where my baby once was. I didn't know I was screaming and crying loudly. My eyes were blinded with tears as I slipped into the darkest time of my life thus far. My mother and father were both praying and reading scriptures from the Bible in this dark time.

EIGHT

Almost a month after the crash, I still found myself standing in the mirror, rubbing my belly, wishing my baby was still there along with Tommy to hold and comfort me. It was hard for me to see him in the casket. The disbelief took over. A part of me was still holding on to him, awaiting a call, at the same time looking at old texts. I missed school for a week until the doctor cleared me. I received a lot of love and support from students who knew Tommy and I. Deborah was also there for me in between living her daily life. Today I was at home waiting on Deborah to come pick me up, because she was having a photo shoot at the Nieman Marcus store with other models, flying in to be there. It was her way of getting me out of the house, to keep my mind occupied. A text came in on my phone. At the same time I could hear the horn blaring.

Deborah: Hurry running late
Angel: Coming now.

I kissed the picture of Tommy before exiting, rushing out to her car. She mashed the gas in a hurry.

"Slow down, please. I want to make it there alive. Plus, you don't want anything to happen to that pretty face of yours," I said.

"I'm running late because Shane wanted to break in our new apartment."

"You have a new place and I'm just now finding out about it?"

"Didn't want to bother you with that, since you've been going through a lot. Besides you're always invited."

"What did your parents think about this move?"

"The age difference isn't a problem. They look at me like a responsible teen anyway. There are three bedrooms, one for my best friend to sleep over, and the other we'll make into a mini sports bar for parties."

"Sounds like you two will have a lot of breaking in to do with three bedrooms," I said.

"When we get to the mall, if you don't want to be bothered or get bored, we can leave," Deborah said.

"Do you see yourself marrying Shane?" I asked, shifting the subject.

My question surprised her, making her briefly glance over at me. "I do love him, if that's what you want to know."

"Enough to get married and have his children

love him? Or is it just fun for now with good sex love him?"

Her eyebrows raised. "We never got that deep. I guess we're allowing each day to bring something new," she said as her cell phone sounded off ringing.

"That's my baby right there," she said, glancing down at the phone.

Right then something came over me, flashing back to when they said Tommy was texting and driving. "Don't do that, crazy! You're going to kill us!" I blurted out, snatching her phone, tapping Ignore, so she could focus on the road. My loud booming voice jolted her to the reality of why I did it.

"I'm sorry, Angel. I'm really sorry. I wasn't thinking."

"No I'm sorry for yelling. I got scared thinking about how Tommy crashed texting on the phone," I said.

"When we get, there I'll have them do your makeup so you can see how sexy and pretty you look," she stated, shifting the topic. I started smiling thinking of how fun it could be to get the makeup treatment she got. "They may even like your curves and biracial skin tone," she added.

It didn't take long before we pulled up. We rushed inside. Someone from the agency noticed her as we entered. "You're late, Ms. Fisher, but beautiful enough not to get fired. Get over there with the rest of the girls. We're on a tight schedule here," the agency rep said. I drifted off, mixing in with those standing around.

A young model came rushing to the area with the other models, bumping into me. "I'm so sorry, super star. I have to take my pictures, but I'll be back to continue apologizing," he said, rushing off, with his light brown skin tone and hazel-green eyes, making him look exotic, backed by the baby face and muscular jawline adding to his features. My eyes somehow followed him over to his set, watching him pose. Then he took his shirt off, displaying his tip-top fitness and chiseled six-pack and ripped biceps, all glistening with oil. He even glanced over at me. I admit he was my type, but my hearty was still with Tommy.

I closed my eyes, turning away, feeling guilty for looking on at him. I opened my eyes and saw him with other male and female models posing. One of the females was Deborah, looking totally different being dolled up for this shoot. Her and the male models were getting close, looking to be intimate, but only for the photo shoot. Her lips were close to his, eyes locked on his, selling the image as the cameras snapped away. As they continued to pose, someone was taking pics and posting them to their Instagram account. From the outside looking in, one would think she was flirting, but I knew she was not.

Shane, on the other hand, was seeing the images being posted, and became jealous, especially with the hashtags attached, further fueling his jealously. Once she was done taking pictures, she was off to the side checking her phone. Her demeanor shifted, smile dissipating. I took my phone out and took pics to show Shane and the world there was nothing going on here but work. A few hours later, we headed out to the car, where Shane was parked alongside of her car.

"Babe what are you doing here?" Deborah asked, since the shoot was over.

"I can't be here now?" he fired back, seeming bothered or insecure.

"You're allowed to be anywhere you please. I meant why did you come late when the shoot is over?"

"I know you're working, but them pics posted had me pissed. I didn't know them dudes was a part of your modeling," he said, looking over at me. "What's up, Angel, you good? I know that was messed up what happened to your boy."

"I'm good. Are you good with my best friend,

because she only loves and wants you. Everything else is work."

"Say no more, Angel. Deborah, you coming home after you drop her off?"

"Yeah, I'll be home right away, to make sure you know you got a good thing," she said, stepping up to kiss him. Then we got into the car and headed to my house.

"Deborah, if he ever gets hands-on with you, I want to know. Has he ever?"

"Not really."

"That's not a good answer. It tells me he has hurt you. I should call the cops on his ass."

"What are you going to tell them? You think he hurt me?" she responded, voice broken as if she was torn between him and the truth.

"Did he hurt you? Don't lie."

"He grabbed me by the arm. He's not stupid to leave marks on my face or anything because I model," she said, trying to minimize his actions, which were not acceptable at any time.

"Why move in with him?"

"He wanted me closer, plus he said he was sorry for grabbing me."

"He will be sorry if he hurts you again. I'll call the cops and get him locked up. Abuse comes in many forms, especially teen abuse."

She became silent taking in my words, knowing she shouldn't tolerate any abuse from anyone. "I promise I won't let anything bad happen to me."

"You better not, because you're my best friend in the whole wide world, and I would go crazy if he hurt you. You know I can come over tonight, for a sleepover," I said, wanting to make sure she was okay.

"Not tonight. I want to have fun with him, so he knows what he has in me. We'll have plenty of time to Netflix and chill," she responded, pulling up to the house.

Her phone was ringing again. It was Shane.

"Really? He's not even going to give you time to drop me off. You should be dating that model guy. At least he wouldn't get jealous of what your day job is."

"The hot guy's name is Dante Brooks. He's a big name in the modeling industry, plus he asked about you. He said you bumped into him."

"No, he almost ran me over to take them sexy

pictures with you and the other models. He apologized and said he would come back."

"And you awaited his return?" Deborah said.

"No, no, that's not what happened." I said. Her phone sounded off again.

"Let me take this call, but before I do, you want me to tell Dante you're interested?"

"No, I'm emotionally unavailable right now, but he is eye candy."

"I'll take that as a yes," she said, answering the call as I exited, heading to the house.

NINE

Close go three months after the conversation with Deborah in the car, she finally came forward about Shane's abuse via text. I was at home eating McDonald's watching TV when the text came through.

Deborah: I hate him sooooo much!!!!

Her words alone spelled it out for me. I put my fries down as my heart started beating in fear for her, my best friend.

Angel: What's going on???
Deborah: Can't stand him right now!
Angel: Did he hit you???
Deborah: Yes! In the face so guys wouldn't look at me!

My heart dropped. I felt helpless in my distance between her and I. I wanted to help.

Angel: I'm calling the cops!!!
Deborah: No need, I already did.
Angel: Where R U?
Deborah: Just got in my car.
Angel: Come to my house.

I didn't know what else to do while I waited on her to get here. I didn't want her texting me back and forth, crying, blurring her vision and distracting her from driving, because if she crashed and bad things happened to her, I wouldn't be able to forgive myself. I was crying, so I knew she was. He hurt my best friend. I exited my bedroom and made my way to my parents' room.

"Mom, Dad, can I speak with you please?" I asked, knowing they would be able to advise Deborah, helping her with her mental and emotional pain.

"What's going on, darling?" my mother asked,

seeing my freshly wiped tears. "Why are you crying?"

"Deborah's boyfriend hit her because he's jealous, thinking that every guy wants her," I said.

"Where is she now, not with him I hope?" The door bell sounded off.

"That might be her. I told her to come over. She needs to be far away from him," I said, knowing what she was going through wasn't love, no matter how many times he said sorry. We headed downstairs together to the front door. When I opened the door to see her bruised face, my knees became weak. "No, no, this isn't right." I cried, opening my arms to welcome her with best friend love, a comforting feeling she needed after being abused. She needed to know it wasn't her fault he hit her.

"Come on in and take a seat. I'll make some warm tea to calm your nerves, and mine too," my mom said as my father was coming down the steps.

My dad, being a strong man, became emotional and upset seeing Deborah's face. "God doesn't like for evil to rise up again his children. This young man, although he looks appealing, is pure evil. No real man does this to God's best creation, a woman," he said, wiping the tear from the corner of his eye before opening his arms to hug her. "Come here, young lady. It's going to be okay. God will take care of those who bring you harm." She cried as she hugged my dad.

"Did he get arrested?" I asked.

"Yes, then they took my picture, and after I saw the medic, for the swelling."

"I don't what you're looking for, young lady, but never accept any form of abuse from anyone. Sorry will never bring you back from the dead. Leave those young men alone until you figure yourself out first," my father said.

I could only imagine what Deborah's father was going to say and do when he saw his princess's marred face. My mother came out with the hot tea, sugar cubes on the side, and a cup of warm milk in case my father wanted it.

"Here you ladies go. Honey, I brought some out for you, too, if you like." Now that we were all seated, I could see this look in Deborah's eyes, showing shock and fear, as if she was sitting there replaying it all over again. She was wincing from the pain too. I rubbed her shoulder, allowing her to know it was going to be okay.

"He can't hurt you anymore. God will see to it," I said, sounding like my parents.

"I have a photo shoot in a few days, and he knew this. These marks and swelling won't be gone by then," Deborah said with her broken voice, partially crying, thinking about her dream of modeling going down the drain, all because of her jealous boyfriend.

"Deborah I know your pain runs deep," my mother said, sipping her tea before continuing, "but God's will is deeper. If they don't understand what has happened to you, then your path will be chose from that decision. Trust and believe what I say to you. God doesn't make any mistakes. That boy didn't appreciate you as Charlie and I do one another. Now he'll be forever regretting his actions for betraying your love and loyalty for him."

Hearing my mother speaking brought a smile to her face, even through the pain she was feeling, especially having a swollen eye. This alone affected her esteem.

"Yeah, Deborah, I hope they give him a lot of time for what he did to you," I said.

"These young kids today listen to music that degrade women, so they try to live up to it, not realizing this isn't what God intended for a man and woman to be, when he created us. He wanted us to procreate and love he another, not abuse and destroy," my father said. "The two of you need to focus on the future, college, and God's plans for each of you. Your happiness will come again. It is already written," he added.

My mom smiled hearing his words, which were spoken from the heart and life experience. "Deborah, if you like, you can stay here tonight?" she offered.

"I want to go home to make my parents aware of this, rather than them reading about it or seeing it on the news," she said, sipping the tea. "I do appreciate you all for your words of wisdom and loving hugs," Deborah added, ready to leave. I gave her a big hug, and my parents did the same.

"No matter what, don't give up on your dreams of modeling. I love you, best friend," I said, wanting to comfort her. Once she left, I turned to my parents. "Thank you for making her feel appreciated and loved with your wise words and direction," I said.

"As parents, whether it is our child or not, it is our duty to give direction, comfort, and love, as God has instilled into us," my father said with his arm around my mother, a true portrait of love.

"One day I, too, will have this love and wisdom to share," I thought, with a smile on my face.

TEN

God's plan, as my father always said, worked for Deborah. A week after the domestic abuse on Deborah, the modeling agency took advantage of this, to expose domestic abuse. They did a photo shoot with her marred face. Then a few months later, when she was 100 percent, they took even more pictures, this time with a male model, making them look like a couple. The caption in Vogue magazine read: "This is how to love." Then on the same page split image, showing the same model standing over Deborah with her battered face, the caption read: "This is not love." The article attached gave Deborah a voice along with other models, male and female, that had gone through a form of domestic abuse. Each of them used their fame to be advocates against domestic violence.

Two years later, Deborah's notoriety as a model and spokeswoman had grown, giving her global fame. We spent the remaining time in high school single. Me, because I needed time to get over Tommy, and Deborah just didn't have time, physically or emotionally. Now going to Penn State University, I found a liking for a quarterback, Tyler Thompson, a six-foot-two, muscularly built hunk of chocolate, with brown skin that seemed to glow under the light, just like his light brown eyes and illuminating smile, which is luring, adding to his charm. All the girls wanted him, but he slowed down enough to pay attention to me in passing, plus we chat online, finding out more about one another. This dating process after not being in the loop felt like staring all over again, being a virgin. I embraced the teenage crush feeling I got when he sent me messages and pics. Today as I was standing at my locker, he came up from behind. I could smell his Sean Jean cologne, Unforgiveable.

"You always smell good," I said, briefly closing my eyes and appreciating his presence.

"I tried to surprise you, but the cologne gave me away."

"That's a good thing. At least you don't have bad breath that will give you away like some people we know."

"I got you a Valentine's Day card," he said, handing me the card. "It would be nice to take you out on a date, so I can further show you my appreciation," he added. I wondered what he had in mind. We'd been talking for a few months now, and we hadn't even kissed yet, thanks to his patience. I wanted to also make sure he wasn't just trying to hit it and quit it, as everyone said most athletes in college did, just because they could with all of the girls flocking behind them.

"It sounds good. What do you have in mind?" I asked, not realizing that lured by his eyes, I started gravitating toward him. He leaned in, finding my lips, so warm and long-awaited, no guilt, just pleasure in this moment. I could taste the banana Now & Later flavor on his tongue and lips, adding to the memory of our first kiss. My hands wrapped around him pulling him closer to me, until I heard my best friend's voice.

"They have hotels for this, you know," Deborah said.

"Don't be hating. You know how long I waited for this kiss," Tyler said with a big smile.

Deborah cut her eyes over at me. "Months for a kiss? You were holding out because you're thinking about joining a convent or something?" Deborah said, being funny and making us laugh.

"Whatever, I'm in my own lane right now," I said, knowing the time I took made this kiss special and worth it.

"You're not the only one that found someone. A certain New York rapper with back-to-back platinum hits sent me a few DMs. We have a trip to Milan scheduled," she said, full of excitement.

"I'm happy for you, details and pics when you

get there," I said, knowing we were growing up and soon we'd be living our own busy lives.

"I guess I'll be waiting a few months to get all the details with this situation at the rate you're going," Deborah said being outspoken as always. "You better be good to my best friend, or you'll lose a good thing and regret it."

"I know what I have. She is nothing like the other girls. She stands out," Tyler responded.

"You two take care of yourself. I have to go. I'll send pics of the show I just did too," Deborah said, hugging me.

"Love ya. Make sure you keep the groupies away from your platinum rapper. That's not a healthy environment for you," I said as she was walking away.

"Now back to you, Angel. What time would you like me to pick you up for dinner?"

"Six will be fine. It'll give me time to get and be ready. You know how us ladies like to make sure what we're wearing fits and looks good," I said.

"Good, I made reservations at Davino's Italian cuisine."

"Sounds good, I haven't eaten Italian food in awhile."

"There's going to be more than Italian food. I don't want to give it all away," he responded, tweaking my interest. I leaned in for another banana Now & Later-flavored kiss. Yes, it was as good as the first kiss.

"I'll see you then," I said after parting from the kiss, watching him walk away with confidence and a nice firm ass from working out.

6:20 PM

Tyler spent the last twenty minutes arguing with the maître d' at the restaurant for giving someone else his reservation. They had given it up to one of the local politicians, who had more public ranking than my boyfriend and star quarterback.

"Tyler, we don't have to let these assholes ruin our Valentine's Day," I said not wanting him to get upset to the point it ruined our evening.

"I wanted this to be special for you, but they messed it up."

"As long as we're together, it is special," I said, wanting him to feel good about this night.

He drove for a few miles before pulling up to a pizza place. "I did say I was taking you for Italian cuisine," he said, making me laugh as he pointed to the sign. He exited the car and came around to open my door. "My lady, welcome to Ricardo's, the best place to spend Valentine's Day, because we do pizza in heart shapes," he said, making me laugh even more. I couldn't ask for a better night, even with the original plans being ruined.

"Heart-shaped pizza, I'm looking forward to that. Does it come with a glass of wine?" I said, going along with his role-play.

"Ah ha, that was a part of the special night for you and me," he said, going in the trunk of his Audi A6, and retrieving a bottle of Nissley Merlot, a Pennsylvania-based wine. He displayed the bottle with a smile, before taking my hand and leading me into the pizza place. We placed our order, a large pepperoni with spicy garlic wings on the side. It was funny how we were both dressed for an upscale dining, yet were here at a pizza joint. We enjoyed our time together along with the pizza and wings, talking, bonding, and staring into each other's eyes.

After dinner we made our way back to the car. The radio played R&B music, setting the mood. We found one another's lips in the process, His touch was also affectionate, resting on my thigh. "No need to rush, the gift is worth the reward of patience," I was thinking. Yet respecting the gentleman side of him, I pulled back from the heated kiss. "It's still early. Where are we going next?" I asked, not wanting our date to end just yet, or that good feeling I was having from the kiss.

"We can go to my dorm, since my roommates are

all out for the night," he responded. I didn't say a word, but my eyes and smile spoke volumes, along with my hand on the tops of his. Once back at his dorm, he turned the TV on, then the music low, before retrieving a bottle of Peach Cîroc he had stashed away. He poured some for me and him. "Happy Valentine's Day, beautiful. This toast is to a good night and making memories," he said.

We locked eyes before downing the drinks. I was already buzzing from the wine we finished off, now this. I was feeling really good. He sat next to me, closing in for a kiss, my hand finding his firm chest, almost as if to control the situation I wanted more of, since his firm chest was making me want to know more about his body. My hand slid over to his masculine arms. The fluttering feeling in my heart was taking place.

This wasn't my first time, but that feeling was occurring as his hands started to roam over my body, finding my breast, tweaking my nipples, making my breathing pick up as my body was being turned on more and more by the second, reacting to his touch. His other hand slid up my leg until he reached my V, caressing it through my tight jeans, stimulating me, making me want to be freed from these clothes that were hindering his touch. I took my hand, undoing the button to my pants, allowing him to slip his hand in and find me. My heart was thumping as soon as his long, thick fingers slid over my pearl, stimulating all of me, parting my flesh, entering slowly, filling up my tightness that hadn't seen action for over two years.

"Mmmmmmh, Mmmmmmh, it's been awhile," I let out. He paused, being gentle, removing my pants, then his. I assisted him out of his shirt, exposing the body of a Greek god chiseled to perfection. His fully erect body was longer and thicker than I'd ever seen, since I only had one other person to compare it to. As he closed in, I took hold of his love stick, guiding him into my body. I squirmed, breathing heavy and moaning. "Oooooh, let me do this, baby, mmmmh," I said sensing he wanted to thrust inside of me. I guided him all the way in as I wrapped my legs around him. "Oooooh, Oooooh, ooooh my, this is different. Mmmmmmh." My moans expressed how his love stick was filling me up, touching all of my insides, making my body come alive. This long-awaited feeling that had been backed up was wanting to be released with each deep stroke. I was feeling the orgasmic sensation bouncing around, rushing through my body. "Aaaaah, oooh my God. Oooooooooh God, mmmmmmmmh." Intense surging was soaring through my flesh with his deep, fast motion picking up, thrusting side to side. He found my place of orgasmic pleasure, and I couldn't hold it back anymore. It was racing through my body, erupting with intense pleasure. "Ooooh, mmm-mmmh, mmmmmmh. I, I, I'm coming. Mmm-mmmh." "OMG," I was thinking in this intense moment of pleasure.

Now his lips were up against my ear, whispering, "I love you, Angel. You are worth every day I waited for this special moment." My heart started fluttering, my body started reacting even more, like his deep strokes matched his words. I became emotional, allowing my body and heart to be his. The orgasmic wave streaming through my body added to the intense moment of pleasure and emotional happiness.

"Mmmmh, mmmmmmh. I, I love you too, mmmmh." Damn, this was a good feeling to have right now. Our session came to a slow halt as our words exchanged, both of us acknowledging the fact we said "I love you" during sex. We made sure it was not just for the moment. Our moment of love and passion really came to an end when we heard his roommates coming through the door. We jumped up, getting our clothes on, but not fast enough.

"Aye, bro, looks like we came in time for the party," Tyler's roommate Mitch said.

"Dude, this is no party over here. She's my girl. So show her some respect. I thought you were all staying out late?" Tyler said.

"You know how it is, bro. We came home to do a little gaming and drinking," he said, referring to the PS5 game by the TV. His other roommates stood there chugging beers. We got ourselves together and stepped out for more privacy.

"Angel, I hope this Valentine's Day started and ended memorably for you," Tyler said.

"I'll never forget this night, or the one I shared it with," I said, looking up at him with a glow in my eyes and in my smile. "We could have gotten a round two in if it wasn't for your roommates, but I look forward to next time," I added, kissing him. We parted from the kiss taking in one another.

"I love and appreciate the visions I have of catering to you," he said, making my heart smile. "I know you don't like to say goodbye, so take care," he added. He watched me walk away strutting, bouncing my filled-out figure, right cheek, left cheek, for his eyes only. I looked over my shoulder blowing him a kiss as I vanished.

ELEVEN

Months had passed now, with Tyler and I becoming more serious, especially with our intimate sessions making me discover more about my body, as well as this growing attraction I had for him each day. We pretty much had a daily routine of communication, face-to-face, emails, and video messages, until I picked up on something that stood out to me. I didn't want to be the jealous type, especially with him being a star quarterback, recording plenty of TV time during games and inter-views. But the second time around, my female instincts kicked in, forcing me to look into what I believed was him giving someone else his attention, only because he canceled our date last minute. As always

I had to include my best friend, just in case she wanted to talk me out of it. I sent a text to Deborah.

Angel: I think he's cheating???
Deborah: I can't w/men right now.

Damn, her response seemed too filled with her own anger and issues. Maybe it was the recent break-up that was public between her and the platinum rapper, who was filmed in sexual acts with his groupies. She was so pissed she burned his race car-red Ferrari.

Angel: I think he has someone @ his place. Should I investigate???
Deborah: UR heart is on the line. Yes!!
Angel: I don't want 2 B right
Deborah: That's the luv U have 4 him in UR heart. But don't B stupid, or blinded by luv
Angel: I luv U best friend, wish me luck
Deborah: I luv you too, but this isn't about luck, it's fate taking its course.

After reading her last message, my mind started

racing, thinking about fate. What if this changed everything? He would never trust me, knowing I was checking after him, especially if he wasn't doing anything. No one wanted to be in a relationship with an insecure woman. I scrolled through my phone looking at pictures of Tyler and me looking so cute together. "Please don't be a scum bag," I said, kissing the photo.

Now my heart was racing, because I was close to his dorm and his room. As I took each step, so many thoughts and scenarios are ran through my head. I finally made it to his door, and I stood there thinking, "Why am I here?" At the same time I prepared to just turn back around and keep the faith and trust in our love. Call me crazy, but when I turned around to leave, I could have sworn I heard him and a female laughing. Without hesitation, I turned the knob on the door, moving silently. I moved through the room, no one in sight. I stood quietly, regretting my actions, until I heard a light giggle once more. My heart started pounding and racing as fast as my mind.

I started toward his bedroom. When I came to the entrance of the room, my feet froze in place, as all the love for him left my flesh, witnessing his infidelity toward our love and relationship. I could only watch him cheating, even though I wanted to look away and run out of the dorm. He was in bed lying on top of his roommate Chad, screwing him in the ass as Chad lay there with his eyes closed, moaning like a female. Tyler, unaware of my presence, was making love to him as he would me. I couldn't understand why he would do this to me. I let him fuck me in my ass. This was insane, I was thinking, until Chad opened his eyes, looking on at me while moaning, not even surprised that I caught them. In fact, I thought he wanted this to happen so Tyler didn't have to keep his sexual preference a secret anymore. Tyler came to a finish and leaned in, kissing on Chad's neck and body just as he had done with me. Now I was feeling violated and betrayed.

"We have a special guest watching us perform," Chad said in a diva tone, with a sadistic smirk on his face. Tyler turned and saw me standing there frozen in the emotional and mental torment of heartbreak.

"Baby, baby, it's not what it looks like," he said, jumping out of the bed.

"Don't fucking baby me! I'm not your baby, your woman, or nothing to you anymore! You want Chad, be with him. Don't string me along, or lie about who you are!" I shouted. He ignored my words and anger, until I kicked him in his shitty dick. Then I turned and ran out of the dorm until I was outside crying by myself, thinking, and "Am I not good enough for love?"

As crazy as he was, he got dressed and ran after me, to no avail, because I didn't want him in my presence. "Get the hell away from me! I hate you! I hate you so much right now!" I said, running away from him. He didn't follow this time, knowing that there was no repairing this damaged relationship. The only thing he was truly concerned about was his image, me exposing his true identity. I was not the type to judge people or blast them by outing them on social media as most would have done already. As my father once said, the decision people make sets the path for us, as it was written by God.

I ran to my car and got into the backseat. I was screaming so loud, feeling this ultimate betrayal, feeling humiliated for loving the wrong person, I missed the first message from Deborah. Now I was thinking to myself, "How am I going to explain to my best friend that my man has left me for another man?" The thought of saying it was painful, making me reflect back to the tormenting images of his betrayal. I ignored the text and incoming calls. I had no words for anyone at this point; my pain was overwhelming me.

I didn't realize I was in the backseat of my car crying for over an hour until a knock came across the back window. I was thinking it was Tyler wanting to assure things would be intact with his image and secret side life. However, it was my crazy best friend looking worried and concerned for my well-being since I didn't return her calls. She thought something bad happened to me physically. She opened the door.

"Really? You're going to just hide in here forever? I know he did you wrong, because he called me trying to get me to side with him, talking about it's not what it seems," she said sitting in the backseat with me.

"Deborah, he was making out with his roommate Chad."

"He didn't tell me what happened," Deborah said.

"He's embarrassed, that's why. He was literally screwing his roommate and didn't even know I was watching them until Chad said something. Seeing that made me feel like shit, as if I'm not enough," I said, crying even more at the image.

"No, no, not big sexy-ass Chad?" she asked in disbelief.

"It hurts so bad, because I let him do things sexually to my body I never had done. What's wrong with me?" I cried out, eyes blurry.

"Nothing is wrong with you. I should go kick his ass for deceiving you. It is his loss, not yours. He better be glad I wasn't there, filming it then putting it on the Gram," Deborah said, angered by what he'd done. I was glad she wasn't there, because I didn't think her filming him and outing him was the right thing to do.

"He chased after me like I was going to let him

continue deceiving me. Can you imagine if his teammates found out about him?" I said.

"Especially the center since he has to stick his hands underneath him every play," she said, making me laugh through the pain. "You want to put him on blast for that, to put him in the pain you're feeling? You know I have fans on Instagram, Twitter, and Facebook."

"No, no, like the first lady once said, when they go low, you go high," I said, not believing in that tit for tat childish behavior.

"Since we're not going to plot revenge, we can't sit in the backseat all night. We both have classes to attend in the morning, and we only have a few hours of sleep to get."

"Thank you for coming to my rescue, because I

would have cried myself to sleep out here, missing all the morning classes," I said, exiting the car and over my aching heart. We started walking back to my dorm.

"My dad told me after I broke up with the platinum rapper that the pain that comes into your life will make you appreciate the true love when it comes into your life. The one love you cherish and always hold onto," Deborah said then added, "I just hope we don't have to go through too many men to find that love or Mr. Right."

"Well, for now, I'm done with looking. My heart can't take any more deception," I said, crushed by what had taken place. I really loved Tyler. He was my rock, my everything. How did I even bounce back from this? "Can you imagine never finding the one because of guys like Tyler and the rapper always seeming to want more?" I said. Before she could even answer, we ran into Tyler, looking distraught in the hall.

"Angel, can I please have one minute with you?" he begged.

"She gave you more than one minute, and you ruined it, dumbass!" Deborah said as we continued on. Like she said, I gave him more than a minute. Truth be told, I would have liked to know if for one second of the many minutes I gave him, he even loved me, or if was I a cover-up for who he really was. I would never know or give him the time to find out.

TWELVE

O ver the next four to five weeks, I was going through an emotional and mental healing process, sometimes crying as if I was not good enough or the problem. Tyler tried to make attempts to get back with me, to no avail. He even broke it off with Chad in fear he would soon be exposed. Not by me, I assured him.

When I finally told my father about this good man doing as he had done to me, my father quoted from the Bible, "Thou shall not lie with man as he does woman. Thou shall not lay with beast as he does woman." I never knew the Bible said that in Leviticus. I thought the beast part was funny. I didn't judge people; that was God's thing. Deborah had also made me laugh with her comment about nuns not having the problems we do with men and love.

The good thing about the breakup was I had more time to focus 100 percent of my attention on college and getting a degree, in between taking trips home to visit my parents and best friend, who was also in town from her worldly travels. The good thing about going back home was my bedroom of childhood memories. I even had a chance to look through old letters and pictures—pictures of Deborah and I being silly, Tommy when we first met two weeks before his demise. As I was looking through the pictures going down memory lane, a text came through from Deborah.

Deborah: Ladies night @ Rumors Night Club.

The two-floor establishment always had crowds

packing the place, especially on ladies' night. Guys would come knowing it would be packed full of women. I'm down for it, a night away from lying and cheating men and their ways.

Angel: Fake IDs or no?
Deborah: I know a guy
Angel: Model life huh? I said referring to her fame.
Deborah: B ready @ 8PM
Angel: C U then.

8:50 PM

I was dressed in my white Prada jeans and red Dior top that was flowing with my red lipstick, making me look extra cute, along with my three-inch pumps by Cavalli and french-manicured nails. I looked and felt good tonight. I appreciated all of me, since there was no man worthy of all of this right now. I looked in the mirror and smiled back at myself, looking at each angle just in case I did run across Mr. Right. I blew myself a kiss before heading downstairs to meet up with Deborah, who should be out front by now.

As soon as I exited the house, she was driving up in a G55 AMG Mercedes Benz truck. I got into the truck seeing my best friend looking like she just came off the runway, wearing her Versace shades and light blue jeans by YSL flowing with her white Versace top with a gold print on the left side.

"Damn, I thought I was looking sexy as hell until the runway model showed up," I said as she tapped the gas and drove off.

"This is our night, no drama, no guys trying to lie to us or get in our pants, just drinks, laughter and memories, all-guy-free zone."

It didn't take long before we were pulling up at

the club and seeing how crowded it was. When we stepped out of the truck looking like video vixens, guys started whistling at us. "Look at the hounds waiting on drunken prey to exit the bar," Deborah said.

"Yeah, horny single woman looking to get some," I said as we came up to the door.

The bouncer recognized Deborah. He waved her and I in. Once inside the club we headed straight to the bar for drinks.

"Let's start it off with shots of apple Cîroc," Deborah said, waving to the bartender and getting immediate service once he recognized her.

"What can I do for you ladies tonight?"

"Two double shots of apple Cîroc, no ice please," Deborah said as I was looking around seeing the guys and ladies dancing together and some alone just enjoying the night out.

"Here's your drinks. Are you running a tab?" the bartender asked. She drank her shot then nudged me to do the same. I followed, not wanting to be the one with the full glass.

"Yes, a tab. Give me two Long Island iced teas, and make them good too," she said. I wiped the corner of my mouth since I rushed to drink the shot. I even forgot how the warmth of vodka was since I hadn't drank since the breakup.

The bartender came back fast with our Long Island ice teas, with the lemon on the rim of the glass. The buzz from the double shot was kicking in as Drake's new song came on blaring through the speakers making me and Deborah start dancing with our drinks in hand. This Long Island was tasting just like regular tea. I could drink a couple of these things.

Almost ruining our mood, a big bouncer came over to us. "No glasses on the dance floor, ladies," he said, directing us from the dance floor. This bouncer was at least six foot nine and 300 muscular pounds. He could easily pick me and Deborah up and toss us out, so we moved quickly off the floor.

It didn't take long before a guy tried to come talk to us. "Hey, sexy lady," he said.

Deborah cut right into him. "Nope, not tonight, my friend. This is a guy-free zone tonight," she said. I admit he was good looking and would have had all of my attention any other time, but like my best friend said, it was ladies' night. He walked away drinking his beer. At the same time we finished our tea. "Two more Long Islands please," she yelled out. This time when the drinks came, we made our way to the other side of the club, to a corner booth, where a server came over.

"What are you ladies eating tonight?" he asked, ready to take down our order.

"Finger food, french fries, wings, sliders, a little of each," Deborah said. "I already have an open tab with the bar. Merge it together," she said, sliding her credit card across the table.

"OMG, Deborah Fisher, I did not know it was you. My little sister is obsessed with you. She wants to be you," the server said. "Oh, I'm sorry. This is not professional."

"It's okay. You're not being weird or anything," she said.

"Can I take this selfie so I can send it to her?"

"Yes, hashtag 'Dreams do come true,'" Deborah responded. After the server left, I looked on at my friend who was just Deborah to me but a star to others. We sat back drinking, waiting on the food to come in between looking on at the eye candy of young men.

"I see a lot of sexy guys in here tonight that would be willing to take us home, but when they wake up in the morning, how long will we want them to stick around, if they're not who we thought they were?" Deborah said, feeling the buzz from the drinks, specially the Long Island iced tea. Truth be told everyone wants love, but no one wants to go through the pain it brings when it doesn't work. Kind of like everyone wanting to go to heaven, but no one wanting to die. How crazy is that?

"I want good love, good sex, and someone I can wake up to every morning and not want to kick them because of their secrets and lies," I said.

"We both need a Tommy Roland in our lives," Deborah said, knowing he was everything to me. A really good boyfriend that understood the value of a relationship.

I shifted the topic, not wanting to go to a sad place thinking back to him. "Let's enjoy tonight and this good food. Look at that sexy beast over there," I said, directing her attention to the guy dancing, gyrating his hips while lifting up his shirt slightly, exposing his cut abs.

She was smiling, eating her food, and starring just like other women in the club. "He's definitely not leaving alone tonight," Deborah said, stuffing her mouth with fries. One would never know she had an appetite like that being a model. We finished the food and continued drinking and laughing the night away.

"Angel Renee, I love you, because you're always the best friend in the whole world. The guys that screwed us over messed up and missed out on our love. They don't deserve this love we have to give," she said, feeling the alcohol buzzing through her body. At the same time she placed her hand on my leg, looking into my eyes. I understood and felt every word she said, because we had been through a lot emotionally. Without question she was my best friend and I loved her, but her hand, her touch, the warmth of this moment and the love in her words were all making me feel this affection deep in my body, catching me off guard, because my hand found the top of hers. The warmth, the silence between us. I could see in her eyes, she loved me differently. However, those brief thoughts came to an abrupt end as we pulled back, looking the opposite way before finishing off our drinks. My heart was fluttering. My mind was confused. Was it the alcohol? I never in my life had looked at her like this, nor had I ever desired to be with another female. In the midst of staring out at the dance floor, I laughed, reflecting back to that brief moment.

The night continued on as if nothing ever happened. We danced with guys, giving them some attention. Most of them, knowing who Deborah was, were so excited to dance with her, even the girls taking selfies. The night came to an exciting end with guys giving us their numbers. As we headed out, Deborah yelled out, "Ladies' night, bitches!"

"We needed this night," I said, feeling good and free from the drama and lies. "I love you, best friend, for this fun night," I said as we were walking through the double glass doors that led to the stairs outside.

"I love you too, Angel Renee," she said, stumbling through the door over to me. Instinctively my hands came up, catching her from falling. My right hand was on her belly below her breast, the left hand on the small of her back.

"Are you okay to drive?" I asked with her face and lips inches from mine, her eyes staring back at me.

"I'm okay to do a lot of things. Driving is the easy part," she said before proceeding through the door. I didn't know if was crazy or drunk, because that same emotional feeling came over me with her being that close to many face, as if we were about to kiss. We headed out to the truck.

"Drive safe so we can make it home in one piece," I said. She just smiled, giving me the thumbs-up, starting the truck, mashing the gas, and racing out of the parking lot. She had Future's new music blasting. It was like a party after the party, riding home. I didn't realize being drunk myself, that she had pulled up to her house instead of mine. This only let me know how drunk she was. Thank God we made it here.

"You're home, Angel. I'll see you tomorrow," she said.

I looked at her parents' mansion then back to her.

"You're joking, right? This is your house, crazy. I thought driving was the easy part."

"It was. I didn't crash."

"Turn the truck off. I'll stay here for the night," I said, not knowing if I should be upset or caring as I got out to help her out of the truck. We could have crashed and died, I was thinking. This could never happen again. "We'll call an Uber or Lift next time."

"I'm okay, Angel. I told you driving is the easy part."

"I heard you the first time, but you're not driving anymore. You're home and it's time for bed."

We made it up to her room, and she flopped on the bed. "Don't leave, Angel, stay the night," she said, not realizing I was staying the night. I helped her out of her shoes. She started taking her pants off.

"Hand me my pajamas please," she said trying to get out of bed with one leg in her pants the other out. I tossed her pajamas to her, before turning around to let her put them on. When I turned back around she was under the covers. "Lay on top of the covers like we did when we were younger," she said. I laughed, knowing she was too much right now.

I took my shoes off before lying on the covers. She turned my way, facing me. "Thank you for being a good friend. I really do love you more than you'll ever know," she said. Once again that feeling came over me. At the same time of me trying to process these thoughts and emotions, she leaned in, placing a kiss on my lips. Instantly a fire of passion ignited inside of me, through this kiss I strangely didn't resist. Her lips, tongue, all different from a guy's.

Then it happened. She pulled back, turning over as if nothing ever happened. My heart and mind were racing. My body was turned on from this unexpected explosive kiss I didn't feel guilty about. It felt natural and not forced. I was open to welcoming more of her touch.

"Don't be confused or scared, Deborah. What just happened is meant to be. It's not luck. It's fate taking its course, as you once told me," I said. Hearing me speak made her turn to look at me. Her eyes said a thousand words that made me feel even more at home in this moment with her.

"I never did this before," she said in the softest tone.

"Neither have I, but we both know what our bodies like. More important, we know we love each other. There are no lies or secrets between us," I said.

"Take your clothes off and join me under the covers," she said, flipping the covers back exposing her already nude body of model perfection. She never put the pajamas on; they were snugged right beside her. I came out of my clothes and slid under the covers next to her, looking into her eyes. My heart and mind raced as my body heated up. Her touch activated the flow of my body. Our hands roamed over each other's bodies as our lips locked in this intimate kiss that was better and more emotionally involved now. Our hands discovered each other's body at the same time, finding a paradise of passion. My fingers entered her soft, warm body. Her fingers found me, creating this erotic sensation, touching my pearl as I did hers.

"Oooooh, oooooooh, mmmmmmmmmh," I let out.

Her moans followed. "Aaaah, aaaaaahh. I'll go first," she said as her kisses trailed from my lips, to my neck, over my breast, to my belly, then my side. I was squirming at her feather-like touch, yet moaning, and she hadn't even started yet. I lay on my back as she parted my legs, closing in on my sweet split, her fingers entering as her tongue came in for a taste of my pleasure.

"Ooooh, oooooh. Oooh God, oooooh God, oooo-oh my mmmmmmmmmh." I was moaning with an intensity I'd never experienced in this feminine touch, as if she'd been here with my body, knowing what to do and how to make powerful orgasmic waves stream through my body. She had found a place down there only a woman could find, making my legs shake, my stomach clench, my heart flutter, as the pulsating storm of orgasm escaped.

"Oooooh. Oooooh God, ooooooooh, this feels so good. Ooooooooh God. Ooooh, Deborah I love you. Mmmmmmh."

I couldn't hold it back anymore. I allowed these powerful orgasms to escape, with great sensation surging through my body. I literally felt high off of each orgasm as endorphins were being released in my brain. I was so into it a tear of joy and pleasure slid down my face. This was so good, as I was embracing the flow of sensation leaving my body. Her tongue and fingers came to a slow halt before she came up to lie at my side. I turned to her, wiping her lips before placing a kiss on them.

"You're a loud moaner, which means I was doing

it right," Deborah said, making me laugh.

"That was beyond different. My body was melt-ing at your touch," I said.

"We know our bodies and what places to go to for that feeling we yearn for," she responded, kissing my lips. "Now all you have to do is think about how you want your body to feel, when you go down there," she said lying on her back.

I did as she had done to me, kissing my way down to her perfect landing strip, smelling floral. My fingers slid over her landing strip and pink pearl. My tongue found her already wet love spot, and she let out a light moan. "Aaah." My fingers were now in play, thrusting inside of her as my tongue caressed her pearl gently, finding her place, igniting a euphoric sensation of a woman's touch.

"Aaaaah, aaaaah, Angel baby, aaaaah." Her moans permeated through the air, allowing me to know I was doing it right. My fingers set in place, creating pressure that made more intense pleasure surge through her body. Her legs shook, raising over my shoulders, my tongue going faster over her pearl.

"Mmmmmmh. Ooooh no, this is so good, mmmmmmmmmh. Aaaaah, aaaah. Aaaaah, aaaaah." Her body erupted with orgasmic flow over my fingers and tongue, unable to hold back as she was squirming over the bed trying to embrace the intense pleasure of the orgasms erupting from her body. She was grabbing fistfuls of sheets as the pleasure took over.

"Aaaaah, I can't. Aaaaah, aaaaah, I can't hold it back. Aaaah, aaah, aaah. I love you, Angel," she let out, feeling the passion of explosive orgasms that were taking her body by storm, opening up her heart even more to this new world of love, a love I also felt inside of my heart and body. My fingers came to a halt before I came up to her side. She kissed my still-wet lips with her flavor on them. She didn't mind, lost in the moment. "Angel, I don't ever want to be away from your moments like this. I love you differently now. We found the love we've been searching for in each other," Deborah said, making me crying with joy.

"I love you the same. No one in the world knows me like you do, nor will they compare to this very moment we have right now," I said, leaning over and giving her a passionate kiss, holding her until we fell asleep.

THIRTEEN

8:43 AM

I woke up to the warmth of her body next to mine. She was still asleep looking beautiful, even when she wasn't trying. "I love this person next to me," I thought with a smile on my face, never seeing this between her and I coming. She was my Tommy Roland reincarnated. I placed a kiss to her soft lips.

She opened her eyes, looking at me. "I woke up to make sure this wasn't a dream," she said.

"Good morning to you too, crazy," I said.

"We have to get out of bed and shower," she said, sliding out of the bed nude, looking picturesque and sexy to me. I was looking at her in a different light now.

We both headed into the large shower with jet streams in the wall for added relaxation. We took time washing one another while appreciating the art of our beauty. "Are we going to let the world know about the newfound love of ours?" Deborah asked.

"I say if it is meant to be, let it flow naturally. Now our parents may have a heart attack finding out, but this was written," I said, still washing her body intimately.

"So are we going to be the chicks buying toys or some Fifty Shades stuff or what?" Deborah said, mocking our situation.

"I'll spank and tie you up if you like, or have been a bad girl," I said, going along with her humorous antics. "I am open to making you happy, no matter what it takes," I added.

183

She leaned in, giving me a kiss that assured me she too was willing to do what it took for this newfound love thing. "The crazy thing now is, guys will see us together and want us even more thinking they can get a threesome."

"They had their chance. It's our time now," I responded, genuinely not wanting to ever let her or this feeling go. At the same time my hands came over her breasts washing them. Her hand slid over my belly button, down to my sacred place, just for her. Her touch was welcoming, yet stimulating. "Mm-mmmmh, this is nice," I let out, ready to let my body melt over her fingertips, until we both heard her mother's voice booming through the air.

"Deborah Lynn! Are you out of your mind, parking the truck like that in the driveway?" she said coming into the bedroom, sounding like she was closing in on the bathroom. Deborah hopped out quick wrapping a towel around herself before exiting the bathroom, not wanting her mother to discover us like this. I turned the shower off, so she wouldn't be concerned about why it was running. The crazy thing was, we both were drunk last night, to the point I didn't even realize how she left the truck. Thank God we made it home safely.

After she spoke with her mom she returned to the bathroom with clothes for me to wear. "That was close. I had to give her the keys so she could let my dad out of the garage. I didn't know I parked messed up. You should have said something."

"Really? We should just be thankful we made it home in one piece, Ms. Driving Is the Easy Part," I responded, drying off before putting on the pink sweats and T-shirt she brought in.

My nipples pressed up against the fabric. "You look good, babe," she said, glancing at my tweaked nipples and perky breasts.

"You're looking sexy yourself with the wet hair, like a swimsuit issue," I said.

"Holy shit, I just remembered today is Saturday and I have a meet and greet and shoot. I have to put something sexy on," she said, remembering a thing she had with Victoria's Secret models that were coming in. This could be her chance to walk in a show in Milan.

"Just to be sure, Deborah, are we a thing, or are we just having fun?" I asked, knowing some girls did this only when they were drinking. I'd seen it too many times on reality TV shows and in college.

"We're having fun with this thing called love, and loving every bit of it," she responded, coming closer for a kiss. "I'm yours to keep, so I guess you can call me your personal freak," she said, displaying her humorous side, which I appreciated about her. She continued getting ready for her scheduled event. She left her hair wet and natural looking.

We left, heading to the mall where her appointment was. As we were driving, all I could reflect on was last night, the leap of fate we took together. This could have gone terribly wrong if either of us had thought or felt differently. I was glad that didn't happen; this feeling I was having right now was the best. I loved my best friend. I couldn't want anything else right now.

Deborah was driving with a smile just as I was smiling, appreciating us and what took place last night. "Thank you for always being a good friend and loving me," I said, looking on at her driving.

"Some people fear love because they're afraid of being hurt or losing it. That's not the case for us, because we've been through a lot together, only to find happiness in one another, because the love was already there." She seemed to pause, wincing as before when she was abused, but a little more like a sharp pain hit her.

"Are you okay?" I asked.

"It's a cramp. I need to hydrate since you drained all of my fluids last night," she said, making light of the situation, even through the cramping pain she was feeling.

"Stop to get something to eat and drink before we get there," I said.

• • •

A few hours later, after the show, Deborah and I went shopping in between kissing and heavy caressing inside the dressing rooms in each store. The level of excitement in this was making us gravitate toward one another even more. We even held hands walking through the mall, and most people didn't even bother to take a second look, simply thinking we were just crazy best friends being jovial, or this was the new normal.

"I love you and this new thing of ours," I said, having her up against the mirror in the dressing room.

"No matter where I am in the world traveling, you have me. No guy is going to come between us or this good thing we have. They had their chances," Deborah said, assuring me that this thing we were doing wasn't for fun, it was for real.

"I would really enjoy staying in this dressing room having intimate time with you, but there are people standing outside of the dressing room waiting to get in," I said before kissing her once more. As soon as we exited, there was a couple waiting to try on clothes. Maybe they were listening in on us, but I was not embarrassed one bit. I enjoyed what we were doing in there.

Deborah, being the crazy one, blurted out, "You two should go in there to keep the fire alive." I laughed as we walked away to enjoy the fun the rest of our day, at the same time bonding with my best friend and newfound lover.

FOURTEEN

A year into our relationship, I now knew where my life and heart would be for the rest of my life: with Deborah. I decided to make arrangements at this well-known restaurant, Pesci's. They served the best fresh imported fish on a five-star level. We went there for the evening, looking the part, dressed to impress, with earrings and bracelets and makeup and nails done. I even wore a white Donna Karen dress that hugged my body, showing off my curves. We both wore our matching Rolex watches that had the inscription, "Never take now for granted." They also boasted our names together.

We sat across from one another enjoying the red wine, being ladies, no shots tonight. "One year later, we're still enjoying and appreciating each other's time and space, because we have one another's heart and best interest," I said.

"Aww, babe that is so sweet. It's also a good thing because I would hate to have to find a new best friend after all these years," she said, being her spontaneous and outspoken self. The food came as I simmered in her humor, loving her even more yet ready to make this next step: seafood alfredo made from scratch with prawns and mussels and garnished with a lobster tail, and I ordered escolar prepared with a light creamy garlic and parsley sauce, along with other savory ingredients, that melt over your tongue.

"We still haven't shared this with the world, but I'm ready to let everyone know where my heart is. I know your parents may take it the hardest, but they'll understand," Deborah said, knowing how religious my parents were.

As I was reaching into my Prada clutch, I saw her wincing again in pain. "Would you like some water, babe?" I asked.

"No, why did you ask that? The wine is just fine."

"You just winced again as you've done in the past," I said, wanting her to know I cared about her well-being. She was a strong girl that didn't like to be seen as weak in anyone's eyes, other than when we were intimate, so she played it off.

"I'm not pregnant. We can rule that out," she said, being funny.

I looked down inside my clutch at the gift I had inside for her.

"Excuse me, babe. I have to use the ladies' room," Deborah said, standing from the table and coming over and kissing me on the cheek. This man across from us with his wife was looking on as if he wanted in on the kiss.

As Deborah was walking away, I looked at the staring man and said, "I love that woman."

He turned his attention back to his wife as if he was ashamed of being nosy. A part of me wanted to follow her over to the bathroom to have a brief moment in the dimly lit corner that led to the bathrooms. However, I'd behave. Instead I removed the ring box, opening it, and seeing the four-carat solitary diamond I'd purchased in installments over the last year. She was worth every dime spent. I was so into my thoughts of proposing to her, until I heard an abrupt screaming.

"Oh my God! Help! We need help over here!" a female customer yelled out, scaring the shit out of me and the other customers. I looked over where the voice was coming from, the bathroom area.

"It's your girlfriend!" the husband yelled out.

"This can't be happening," I was thinking as I jumped up and raced over there, only to see her on the floor. "Deborah, wake up, please. Don't do this. Open your eyes," I pleaded, feeling my heart breaking and aching.

Her eyes opened, looking back at me, and she managed to smile. "I'm okay. You're right, I need some water," she said, reaching her hand out for mine. I held it, feeling the love yet fear of losing her at the same time.

"Don't scare me like this. I need you in my life, crazy."

"Did I ruin the night?" she asked.

"No, no, you could never do that."

Medics came just as she blacked out again. I was a total emotional mess wanting her to be all right, at the same time wanting to know what was wrong with her. An hour later she was stabilized, and I was at her bedside reflecting back to the last time I was in a position like this with someone I loved. I sobered up quick as the fear took over. I was also praying for two.

When she opened her eyes, it made me feel my prayer was answered. "This doesn't look, good babe," she said, seeing the IV hooked up to her arm. "I guess they stole my sexy dress too. I wanted that right to be reserved for you at the end of the night, to take it off," she added, making me smile through the fear.

"This isn't a funny matter. We need to find out what's wrong with you," I said as the doctor was coming in.

"Ms. Fisher, I'm Dr. Duvall. I was looking at your chart and blood work. I'm sorry to inform you that it is showing signs of advanced cancer. Now we can run another test—"

"Check it again. This isn't right," I said, not wanting to lose her. He jotted down something on his pad before agreeing to run more tests. In the same instance I flashed back to when my grandfather was diagnosed with cancer. He didn't last much longer after that.

"Deborah, how do you feel?" I asked.

"I feel good, and more important, because of you, I feel loved." I caressed her warm flesh with love hoping she didn't ever leave me. I wouldn't be able to take this much pain losing her. I wanted to show her how I really felt as I retrieved the ring from my meinking.

clutch. I also accessed the music on my phone playing Sade's "Cherish the Day."

Deborah smiled as I came back over to her with the music playing as I started to profess my love to her. The ring was sight now. "Deborah Lynn Fisher, I love you so much and will love you always until our last breath. I want to be your wife and the best part of your day and life, because you bring out the best in me," I said, asking for her hand in marriage, sliding the ring over her finger.

"Angel Renee Waters, there will never be any pain in loving or being loved by you. I take great pleasure in being your wife too," she said as we leaned in for a kiss that was filled with true love and passion. "Now I have to get better, so we can have a big wedding and honeymoon sex," she said.

I couldn't lie, her outspoken ways and words

made me gravitate toward her. "Deborah, in all seriousness, I don't ever want to lose you," I said.

"How can you lose what is in the heart?" she responded, making me understand the truth in our love. I leaned in, kissing her, when I heard a familiar voice coming from behind.

"I never saw this coming," Mr. Fisher said, standing there with his wife, who was looking shocked at us kissing. We parted from the kiss.

"They said you were sick, but I didn't think they meant this way," Mrs. Fisher said, not knowing how to take it.

"We're not just best friends, we love each other intimately," Deborah said, raising her hand and displaying the ring.

Her mom placed her hand over her heart, not knowing how to process it. We went into detail, telling them how we came to this point. Then we discussed the reason for being there in the hospital and what the doctor said. Mr. Fisher wasn't trying to hear it. He stormed out in search of the doctor to get another blood test done. He couldn't stand the thought of losing his baby girl, and neither could I.

"I feel fine, everyone. I'm not going anywhere anytime soon. Now if you like, I can get everyone here some pretty pink pills to make them feel better," Deborah said, trying to divert how she really felt.

"What we need is to make sure you are okay and healthy, so you can continue modeling, because being here with that gown on doesn't look good on you," her mom said.

Her parents sat at her bedside until they dozed off. I was too scared to fall asleep. I lay there in bed with her, looking into her eyes and reflecting back to our lifetime of memories.

"I love you and this ring, Angel. It's beautiful. I will be okay to love you forever," she said, being serious, yet I could see not only the love in her eyes, but also the fear of not being able to fulfill that promise of loving me.

"Touch me, caress me with love," she said as if a darkness was closing in on her. She was tired and ready to fall asleep. I wrapped my arms over her. Deborah being Deborah tried to turn this sad yet loving moment into an intimate one, with her hand sliding up my dress. I feared her parents would awake or a nurse would come in.

"Stop, we can't do this here." I said.

"What if I don't have a chance to do this anymore, to feel your love and body?" she said, finding me. I didn't know whether to moan or cry because of her words and touch. I leaned in with my mouth against her, not wanting to moan loud. "Remember my touch, remember how much I love only you," she whispered, making my heart, mind, and body flutter with passion and affection. We held one another close all night until I finally fell asleep, never wanting what we had to end.

FIFTEEN

I was awakened in the morning by Deborah shoving me. "Get up, babe, we're leaving." I opened my eyes, somewhat confused about what was taking place. Once I focused, I saw she was back in the dress she had on at the restaurant.

"I'm going to sue these assholes for scaring the shit out of me!" she added.

"What's going on?" I asked, sitting up.

"The doctor mixed my chart up with someone else's. The only thing wrong with me is dehydration. I was drinking too much caffeine and not enough water." She didn't have cancer, thank God. Hearing this made me start crying joyful tears. The love of my life was going to live to love me.

"So you're not going to leave me?" I asked, partially in disbelief.

"Not before I have a chance to be bridezilla," she responded.

"Once you get ready, Angel, we'll all head out for breakfast," Mr. Fisher said.

Once we left the hospital I felt even better knowing that she was going to be okay. Now we just had to keep it that way.

"I can't believe I didn't see this proposal coming, or the ring, since we're always together. That was one hell of a secret, Angel."

"A good secret you deserve and earned for winning me over," I said, holding her hand.

"Now that we know I'm okay, I'll thank you for this ring later," she said.

All we wanted to do was make one another happy inside and out. She also used her platform, along with me, to express to the world that people like us didn't need to keep it a secret, meaning their true sexual preference and how they identified. Deborah and I went for a walk after breakfast and getting freshened up for the day. We needed time to be and feel finally free in our own skin and love.

We went to the Italian Lake in Harrisburg. It was a picturesque area with an abundance of flowers and geese gliding across the water.

"This would be a good place to have our wedding," Deborah said.

"I'm open to it. We can say our vows right there on the bridge in between the lake," I said, pointing to it. "Are we both wearing dresses?" I added.

"Yes, because we're two lipstick lesbos and sexy beasts," she said as I took her hand with the ring on it, kissing it as I looked into her eyes.

"Deborah, you are my perfect destination and where I always want to be," I said.

She pulled me close, giving me a kiss before asking. "Do you love me enough to jump in the lake?" I didn't even have a chance to respond before she started taking her clothes off down to her bra and panties. "YOLO! Bra and panties are PG. These kids probably have seen more than that."

I followed behind her, taking my things off. She took my hand, and we both ran toward the water jumping in being adventurous. People were looking on at us as if we were crazy, since this lake wasn't for swimming, only for wildlife and appreciating the art of it.

"You bring the best out in me, Deborah. I never would have done this alone. It's exciting."

"So is loving you. It's full of life and excitement that gives me meaning and motivation to figure out ways to keep you smiling, inside and out," she said, coming over to me. People were staring like we were mermaids or wildlife. Even the kids around were pointing at us. "Let's give them something else to look at," she added, kissing me.

After the kiss we hurried out of the water, especially when some started removing their phones to record and/or call the park ranger. We didn't need that problem, so we left in a hurry. But not fast enough. Some of those with the phones got us together and put it on their IG, since they recognized

Deborah. The hashtag read "the new portrait of love." I thought it was cute. As for the videos of us in the water, they went viral, making her more famous and desired by designers.

Yeah, my love story ends with me still having the greatest feeling in the world, being married to my best friend for five years now. I wouldn't change a thing. I hope my love story inspires you to find your heart's true desires. You, too, deserve this level of emotional happiness, that will comfort you forever.

To order books, please fill out the order form below:
To order films please go to www.good2gofilms.com

Name:_____

Address:_____

City:_____State:_____Zip Code: _____

Phone:_____

Email:_____

Method of Payment: Check   VISA MASTERCARD

Credit Card#:_ _____

Name as it appears on card: _____

Signature: _____

Item Name	Price	Qty	Amount
48 Hours to Die – Silk White	$14.99		
A Hustler's Dream – Ernest Morris	$14.99		
A Hustler's Dream 2 – Ernest Morris	$14.99		
A Thug's Devotion – J. L. Rose and J. M. McMillon	$14.99		
All Eyes on Tommy Gunz – Warren Holloway	$14.99		
Black Reign – Ernest Morris	$14.99		
Bloody Mayhem Down South – Trayvon Jackson	$14.99		
Bloody Mayhem Down South 2 – Trayvon Jackson	$14.99		
Business Is Business – Silk White	$14.99		
Business Is Business 2 – Silk White	$14.99		
Business Is Business 3 – Silk White	$14.99		
Cash In Cash Out – Assa Raymond Baker	$14.99		
Cash In Cash Out 2 – Assa Raymond Baker	$14.99		
Childhood Sweethearts – Jacob Spears	$14.99		
Childhood Sweethearts 2 – Jacob Spears	$14.99		
Childhood Sweethearts 3 – Jacob Spears	$14.99		
Childhood Sweethearts 4 – Jacob Spears	$14.99		
Connected To The Plug – Dwan Marquis Williams	$14.99		
Connected To The Plug 2 – Dwan Marquis Williams	$14.99		
Connected To The Plug 3 – Dwan Williams	$14.99		
Cost of Betrayal – W.C. Holloway	$14.99		
Cost of Betrayal 2 – W.C. Holloway	$14.99		
Deadly Reunion – Ernest Morris	$14.99		
Dream's Life – Assa Raymond Baker	$14.99		
Finding Her Love – Warren C. Holloway	$14.99		
Flipping Numbers – Ernest Morris	$14.99		
Flipping Numbers 2 – Ernest Morris	$14.99		

Forbidden Pleasure – Ernest Morris	$14.99		
He Loves Me, He Loves You Not – Mychea	$14.99		
He Loves Me, He Loves You Not 2 – Mychea	$14.99		
He Loves Me, He Loves You Not 3 – Mychea	$14.99		
He Loves Me, He Loves You Not 4 – Mychea	$14.99		
He Loves Me, He Loves You Not 5 – Mychea	$14.99		
Killing Signs – Ernest Morris	$14.99		
Killing Signs 2 – Ernest Morris	$14.99		
Kings of the Block – Dwan Willams	$14.99		
Kings of the Block 2 – Dwan Willams	$14.99		
Lord of My Land – Jay Morrison	$14.99		
Lost and Turned Out – Ernest Morris	$14.99		
Love & Dedication – W.C. Holloway	$14.99		
Love Hates Violence – De'Wayne Maris	$14.99		
Love Hates Violence 2 – De'Wayne Maris	$14.99		
Love Hates Violence 3 – De'Wayne Maris	$14.99		
Love Hates Violence 4 – De'Wayne Maris	$14.99		
Married To Da Streets – Silk White	$14.99		
M.E.R.C. – Make Every Rep Count Health and Fitness	$14.99		
Mercenary In Love – J.L. Rose & J.L. Turner	$14.99		
Money Make Me Cum – Ernest Morris	$14.99		
My Besties – Asia Hill	$14.99		
My Besties 2 – Asia Hill	$14.99		
My Besties 3 – Asia Hill	$14.99		
My Besties 4 – Asia Hill	$14.99		
My Boyfriend's Wife – Mychea	$14.99		
My Boyfriend's Wife 2 – Mychea	$14.99		
My Brothers Envy – J. L. Rose	$14.99		
My Brothers Envy 2 – J. L. Rose	$14.99		
Naughty Housewives – Ernest Morris	$14.99		
Naughty Housewives 2 – Ernest Morris	$14.99		
Naughty Housewives 3 – Ernest Morris	$14.99		
Naughty Housewives 4 – Ernest Morris	$14.99		
Never Be The Same – Silk White	$14.99		
Scarred Faces – Assa Raymond Baker	$14.99		

Scarred Knuckles – Assa Raymond Baker	$14.99		
Secrets in the Dark – Ernest Morris	$14.99		
Secrets in the Dark 2 – Ernest Morris	$14.99		
Shades of Revenge – Assa Raymond Baker	$14.99		
Slumped – Jason Brent	$14.99		
Someone's Gonna Get It – Mychea	$14.99		
Stranded – Silk White	$14.99		
Supreme & Justice – Ernest Morris	$14.99		
Supreme & Justice 2 – Ernest Morris	$14.99		
Supreme & Justice 3 – Ernest Morris	$14.99		
Tears of a Hustler – Silk White	$14.99		
Tears of a Hustler 2 – Silk White	$14.99		
Tears of a Hustler 3 – Silk White	$14.99		
Tears of a Hustler 4 – Silk White	$14.99		
Tears of a Hustler 5 – Silk White	$14.99		
Tears of a Hustler 6 – Silk White	$14.99		
The Betrayal Within – Ernest Morris	$14.99		
The Last Love Letter – Warren Holloway	$14.99		
The Last Love Letter 2 – Warren Holloway	$14.99		
The Panty Ripper – Reality Way	$14.99		
The Panty Ripper 3 – Reality Way	$14.99		
The Solution – Jay Morrison	$14.99		
The Teflon Queen – Silk White	$14.99		
The Teflon Queen 2 – Silk White	$14.99		
The Teflon Queen 3 – Silk White	$14.99		
The Teflon Queen 4 – Silk White	$14.99		
The Teflon Queen 5 – Silk White	$14.99		
The Teflon Queen 6 – Silk White	$14.99		
The Vacation – Silk White	$14.99		
The Webpage Murder – Ernest Morris	$14.99		
The Webpage Murder 2 – Ernest Morris	$14.99		
Tied To A Boss – J.L. Rose	$14.99		
Tied To A Boss 2 – J.L. Rose	$14.99		
Tied To A Boss 3 – J.L. Rose	$14.99		
Tied To A Boss 4 – J.L. Rose	$14.99		
Tied To A Boss 5 – J.L. Rose	$14.99		

Time Is Money – Silk White	$14.99		
Tomorrow's Not Promised – Robert Torres	$14.99		
Tomorrow's Not Promised 2 – Robert Torres	$14.99		
Two Mask One Heart – Jacob Spears and Trayvon Jackson	$14.99		
Two Mask One Heart 2 – Jacob Spears and Trayvon Jackson	$14.99		
Two Mask One Heart 3 – Jacob Spears and Trayvon Jackson	$14.99		
Wife – Assa Ray Baker & Raneissa Baker	$14.99		
Wife 2 – Assa Ray Baker & Raneissa Baker	$14.99		
Wrong Place Wrong Time – Silk White	$14.99		
Young Goonz – Reality Way	$14.99		
Subtotal:			
Tax:			
Shipping (Free) U.S. Media Mail:			
Total:			

Make Checks Payable To Good2Go Publishing, 7311 W Glass Lane, Laveen, AZ 85339

CPSIA information can be obtained
at www.ICGtesting.com
Printed in the USA
LVHW021804161121
703500LV00014B/410

9 781947 340664